He'd said it was up to her what happened next.

Dani stood outside, frowning, one bare foot poised to take her back to her own room, one hand ready to knock on Teague's door.

It opened suddenly, and Teague stood in the doorway, searching her face. "Are you coming in, or were you planning to stand there all night?"

Her terms, she reminded herself, stiffening her spine. "I was thinking about coming in," she said. "But this is only about now. Tonight. Once we get back to Little Rock, everything will probably go back to the way it was between us."

He shrugged, his gaze roaming down her body and back up to her face. "If tonight's all we've got, then let's not waste any more of it just standing here staring at one another."

But he was so nice to stare at, with his tanned skin and well-defined muscles.

She reached out to him.

"Who's wasting time now?"

D0668642

Dear Reader,

When a new romance idea comes to me, it usually revolves around one couple and their conflict. Occasionally, I've concentrated on a group of siblings or friends, with planned connected books. At other times, I've spun off stories I never intended to tell when secondary characters grabbed my attention.

This happened while I was writing *Finding Family.* Rachel Madison, who fell in love with Dr. Mark Brannon in *Finding Family,* had a trouble-prone younger sister, Dani. The more I got to know Dani, the more interesting she became to me. Dani had a lot of growing up to do— and I realized I'd like to watch her evolve. To further complicate her journey, and to reward her for her efforts, I introduced her to a sexy and lonely FBI agent with an ingrained wariness of pampered princesses.

I had a lot of fun bringing Dani and Agent Teague McCauley together. I hope you, too, enjoy their quest for a partnership that will last for a lifetime.

Gina Wilkins

THE MAN NEXT DOOR

GINA WILKINS

Silhouette®

SPECIAL EDITION®

Published by Silhouette Books

America's Publisher of Contemporary Romance

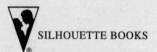

SILHOUETTE BOOKS

ISBN-13: 978-0-373-24905-3
ISBN-10:   0-373-24905-5

THE MAN NEXT DOOR

Copyright © 2008 by Gina Wilkins

Books by Gina Wilkins

Silhouette Special Edition

The Father Next Door #1082
It Could Happen to You #1119
Valentine Baby #1153
§*Her Very Own Family* #1243
§*That First Special Kiss* #1269
Surprise Partners #1318
**The Stranger in Room 205* #1399
**Bachelor Cop Finally Caught?* #1413
**Dateline Matrimony* #1424
The Groom's Stand-In #1460
The Best Man's Plan #1479
The Family Plan #1525

Conflict of Interest #1531
Faith, Hope and Family #1538
Make-Believe Mistletoe #1583
Countdown to Baby #1592
The Homecoming #1652
‡*Adding to the Family* #1712
‡*The Borrowed Ring* #1717
‡*The Road to Reunion* #1735
Love Lessons #1787
The Date Next Door #1799
The Bridesmaid's Gifts #1809
Finding Family #1892
The Man Next Door #1905

Previously published as Gina Ferris:

Silhouette Special Edition

Healing Sympathy #496
Lady Beware #549
In from the Rain #677
Prodigal Father #711
‡*Full of Grace* #793
‡*Hardworking Man* #806
‡*Fair and Wise* #819
‡*Far To Go* #862
‡*Loving and Giving* #879
Babies on Board #913

Previously published as Gina Ferris Wilkins:

Silhouette Special Edition

†*A Man for Mom* #955
†*A Match for Celia* #967
†*A Home for Adam* #980
†*Cody's Fiancée* #1006

§Family Found: Sons & Daughters
‡Family Found
†The Family Way
**Hot Off the Press
*The McClouds of Mississippi

GINA WILKINS

is a bestselling and award-winning author who has written more than seventy novels for Harlequin and Silhouette Books. She credits her successful career in romance to her long, happy marriage and her three "extraordinary" children.

A lifelong resident of central Arkansas, Ms. Wilkins sold her first book to Harlequin Books in 1987 and has been writing full-time since. She has appeared on the Waldenbooks, B. Dalton and *USA TODAY* bestseller lists. She is a three-time recipient of the Maggie Award for Excellence, sponsored by Georgia Romance Writers, and has won several awards from the reviewers of *Romantic Times BOOKreviews*.

For my aunt, the "other" Gerry—
we'll always share a smile over that.

Chapter One

Teague McCauley was so tired his steps dragged as he made his way from the parking lot to his apartment. It was actually an effort to place one foot in front of the other. He could feel his shoulders drooping. Even his dark hair felt limp around his face.

Though he usually took the stairs, he rode the elevator up to his third-floor apartment. He was the only occupant, since most of the other residents had already left for their jobs at eight-forty-five on this Tuesday morning. It would probably be quiet during the day as he got some sleep for the first time in more than forty-eight hours. Not that it would matter. He felt as though he could sleep in a blasting zone right now.

The elevator stopped and he pushed himself away from the wall he'd been leaning against. A few more steps, he reminded himself as the doors began to slide open, and then he could...

At the sight of the woman waiting for the elevator, he snapped instinctively to attention. He pulled his shoulders back, lifted his head and tightened his face into what he hoped was a pleasantly bland expression, nodding as he moved out of her way. "Good morning."

She looked as fresh as a fall chrysanthemum in a bright orange top and crisp brown slacks, her long, glossy brown hair shining around her pretty oval face, her navy-blue eyes cool when she returned the greeting perfunctorily. "Good morning."

"Have a nice day," he said over his shoulder as he strolled away, his steps brisk.

"You, too," she murmured, her reply as meaningless as the clichéd phrase that was all that had popped into his exhaustion-hazed mind.

He heard the elevator doors swish closed behind him, and his back sagged again, his feet almost stumbling the rest of the way to his apartment door. *Yeah,* he thought, fumbling with the key, *you really wowed her with your witty conversation, McCauley.*

Not that it would have mattered if he had come up with even the most clever line. His down-the-hall neighbor had made it very clear during the past few months that she wasn't interested in getting to know him better. Something about the way she practically glowered at him every time she saw him, not to mention the ice that dripped from her tone every time he manipulated her into speaking to him, as he had just then, had given him a clue.

As an FBI agent, he liked to think he was pretty good at reading between the lines that way.

It was a shame, really, he thought, already stripping out of his black T-shirt as he headed straight toward his bedroom without even bothering to turn on lights in the spartanly furnished living room. She certainly was a looker. Face of an angel, body of a goddess. And all the warmth of a snow queen.

Totally out of clichés, he kicked his jeans into a corner, stripped off his socks and fell facedown onto his bed, wearing nothing but navy boxers. He didn't have time for a relationship, anyway, he thought as consciousness began to fade.

Still a shame, though…

Dani Madison waited until she was certain the elevator doors were closed before she released the long breath she'd been holding. It was the same every time she ran into the man who lived in the apartment down the hall. Her breath caught, her pulse tripped, little nerve endings all over her body woke up and started tingling. Very annoying.

Fortunately, she rarely saw him. Maybe a half dozen times total, in the approximately four months since he'd moved in. He wasn't home much, being gone sometimes for more than a week at a time, from what she'd observed. When he was home, it was at strange hours. Like today, just coming in when most people were leaving for work. Looking so tired she'd thought it was a wonder he was standing upright, even though he'd made an obvious, macho effort to hide his exhaustion.

He worked for the FBI. She knew that because he occasionally wore T-shirts with the letters stenciled across his chest. Sometimes he wore suits, and she thought she'd caught a glimpse of a holster beneath his jacket. Maybe that was part of the reason she found him so intriguing.

Well, that and the fact that he was absolutely, positively, heart-stoppingly attractive. Black hair worn a bit shaggy. Gray eyes that looked almost silver at times. Straight, dark eyebrows, neat, midlength sideburns, a jawline that could have been chiseled from granite, but with just a hint of a dimple in his right cheek to add a touch of softness. When he was unshaven, as he had been this morning, he had the look of a

pirate or an Old West lawman. A little wild, a little dangerous—a whole boatload of sexy.

All added together, those things were enough to make her
feel the need to run very hard in the opposite direction every
time she saw him.

Not that he would bother to pursue her if she did, she
thought, shifting her leather tote bag on her shoulder as she
stepped off the elevator. Other than greeting her politely each
time they passed in the hallway, he'd shown no particular
interest in her. Mrs. Parsons, the nosy little old lady who lived
in the apartment next door to hers, directly across from the
man in question, showed more curiosity about her. Agent
Double-O Gorgeous had barely even noticed her.

Exactly the way she wanted things to remain, she assured
herself. She had spent the past fourteen months avoiding any
complicated entanglements with men, most especially the
dangerous-looking ones. And her FBI neighbor sat firmly at
the very top of that list.

It had taken her more than twenty-seven years and a long,
humiliating list of mistakes, but she had finally learned her
lesson, she thought with a sense of accomplishment. Dani
Madison was on her own, independent, self-sufficient, cautious and wisely cynical. It was going to take more than a
rolling swagger and a pair of gleaming silver eyes to change
her back into the naive and affection-hungry girl she had
been before.

Dani hadn't particularly wanted her date to walk her to her
door the next Friday night, but he insisted on doing the gentle-
manly thing and seeing her safely inside. Maybe he hoped
she'd have a last-minute urge to invite him in, but that wasn't
going to happen, she thought as they stepped off the elevator.

Anthony was a nice guy, in an accountant-next-door sort of way, but he set off no sparks in her at all.

Not that she was looking for sparks, really. A pleasant dinner with conversation that ranked somewhere above the entertainment level of the average television program was all she wanted from her escorts these days. Anthony had certainly provided the former, treating her to a meal in a very nice Italian restaurant. As for the latter—well, their dinnertime discussion had been only marginally more interesting than the latest episode of the medical drama she'd have watched had she stayed at home alone that evening.

Agent Sexy stepped out of his apartment down the hall just as she and Anthony reached her door. Too aware of her neighbor strolling toward the elevators, she smiled up at her companion and said briskly, "Thank you again for the meal, Anthony. I had a very nice time."

He glanced wistfully at the doorknob in her hand. "I've had a good time, too. I hate for the evening to end so soon."

"Yes, well, I have an early class in the morning and I have some preparation to do for it."

The apartment door next to Dani's opened a crack and a curious face peered out past the security chain. Dani knew old Mrs. Parsons had heard noises and was checking to see what was going on. The elderly woman was pleasant enough, but boredom made her intensely interested in everything that went on in the apartments around her. Seeing Dani looking back at her, she smiled sheepishly and closed the door again.

FBI guy had pushed the elevator button and was waiting patiently for it to arrive. If he was even aware of Dani and Anthony standing only a few yards away, he'd given no sign of it. Nor did Anthony seem to notice the other man as he nodded resignedly in response to Dani's excuse for not inviting him in. "I understand. Maybe we can get together sometime next weekend? Go to a movie or something?"

"I'm not sure of my plans for next weekend. Why don't you give me a call later in the week."

Anthony's expression fell even more. Maybe he'd read the lack of enthusiasm in her expression a bit too well. "Okay. So, uh, see you, okay?"

She tried to add a bit of warmth to her smile. She didn't want to hurt the guy's feelings. She just didn't want to lead him on, either. "Good night, Anthony."

He leaned over to give her a somewhat awkward kiss on the lips, which she allowed to last only long enough for courtesy's sake. And then she drew away and opened her door. "Good night," she said again.

"Good night, Dani."

The elevator doors opened just as she stepped inside her apartment. She heard Anthony call out, "Hold the car, please."

She closed her door without waiting to see if her neighbor had complied with the request.

High maintenance. Definitely the type who expected men to cater to her wishes. Exactly the kind of woman Teague preferred to avoid, even if they happened to be beautiful—which that sort generally was.

Having ridden the elevator down with his attractive neighbor's latest dejected suitor only the night before, Teague was even more convinced now that asking her out would be a bad idea, despite the temptation to do so every time he passed her in the hallway.

He wasn't proud of the fact that he'd chosen to wait for the elevator rather than take the stairs only because he'd been curious about how her evening with her hopeful escort would end. Or that he'd found some satisfaction in watching her send the other guy on his way.

Physical attraction, he assured himself, strolling into his office at FBI headquarters in western Little Rock Saturday morning. That was all there was to it. Any red-blooded male would be interested in Danielle Madison—for he'd learned that was her name. Apparently, she answered to the nickname of Dani, which was what her date had called her when he'd told her good-night.

He'd only bothered to find out her name for the sake of idle curiosity, of course. It was wise for a man in his line of work to have general information about those who lived close to him. So, while making an effort to discover Dani's name, he'd learned those of the others nearest to him, as well.

There were four apartments on either side of the bank of elevators in the center of the apartment building, two apartments on each side of the hallway. His place was across from Edna Parsons, a widow who rarely left her apartment. The apartment next to his had been occupied for the past couple of months by a studious-looking woman in her midtwenties who seemed pleasant enough but wasn't home much more than he was. The few times he'd seen her, she'd carried a heavy-looking backpack, so he assumed she was a student. Her name was Hannah Ross.

Directly across from Hannah lived Danielle Madison, the striking brunette he had mentally dubbed "The Princess" when he'd moved in and spotted her for the first time.

Hanging his jacket on the back of his chair, he settled at his desk and booted up his computer. He had a lot to do that day, entirely too much to waste any more time thinking about Danielle.

Maybe he should call one of his casual women friends this

weekend. He'd been working too hard lately, hadn't even had a dinner date in a couple of months. Like now, doing paperwork on a Saturday after being in on a sting operation until just after midnight the night before.

That probably explained why he'd spent so much time thinking about his neighbor. A simple matter of hormones too long ignored.

He couldn't help chuckling, though, when he remembered how doleful that guy in the elevator had looked after being literally kissed off by Danielle. What a schmuck.

"So, what's so funny? You're the only guy I know who'd spend a Saturday in the office grinning over his paperwork."

Looking up in response to the lazy drawl, Teague watched as his friend and associate Mike Ferguson slouched into the room. Slouching was pretty much Mike's primary posture choice. Tall and lanky with a mop of curly hair that couldn't decide whether it was brown or blond, he leaned, slumped, sprawled or flopped, but rarely stood at full attention. He claimed it was a lingering rebellion from his years in the military.

Teague shrugged in response to Mike's question. "Oh, I was just thinking about this girl I know. Well, sort of know. Actually, I don't know her at all."

"But she still makes you smile over paperwork?" Mike dropped into a straight-backed chair—the only place to sit in the minuscule office other than Teague's desk chair—and grinned quizzically at him. "Sounds like someone you'll want to get to know."

"Nah. High maintenance. Only dates drooling lap dogs."

Mike shuddered. "Spare me from the princesses."

"Yeah. That's what I call her. To myself, of course."

"She's hot?"

"Let's just say that sprinkler systems go off when she walks down the hall."

"Man."

"Yeah. Real waste."

"Maybe just one date?"

Teague chuckled and shook his head. "Not worth it. She might look hot, but she's cold as ice. And she glares at me as if I might carry Ebola or something. I'll just settle for looking."

Mike tsked sympathetically. "You want to go to Snuffy's tonight? Might find someone there who'd let you do more than look."

After giving it a moment's thought, Teague shrugged. Hadn't he just been telling himself he needed to get out more? Do a little opposite-gender socializing? "Sure, why not? I've just got to wade through this paperwork first."

"How long's that going to take?"

"Four, five hours," he replied glumly.

Because he knew his co-worker wasn't exaggerating, Mike nodded, stood and ambled toward the office door. "Just head over to Snuffy's later, when you're ready. We'll meet up there."

Putting hands to keyboard, Teague ordered himself to focus on work. He'd have a good time tonight, he promised himself. Thoughts of the ice princess down the hall wouldn't even cross his mind.

By coincidence, Dani drove into her parking space at almost exactly the same time Agent Sexy pulled into his own space late Saturday afternoon. She locked her aging compact SUV even as he pushed the button on the remote lock to his small black sports car. They moved toward their apartment building at the same time, reaching the door simultaneously. Nodding pleasantly, her neighbor held the door for her.

Tucking her large canvas tote bag under her arm, she murmured a thank-you and stepped past him. They strolled together down the hallway. Expecting the guy to take the stairs, as was his habit from what she had observed—only coincidentally, of course—Dani stopped to press the elevator button for herself.

She was rather surprised when Agent Sexy stopped with her.

"Long day," he explained, as if noting the question in her expression. "Stairs just seem like too much trouble right now."

She nodded and glanced up at the illuminated numbers, noting that the elevator was stopped on the fourth floor. *Come on,* she thought. *Hurry up.*

"You know, I moved in here almost four months ago, and I've never introduced myself to you," he said conversationally. "I'm Teague McCauley."

So now she had his name. Yet something told her she would still think of him as Agent Sexy.

"Nice to meet you," she said, because she was expected to respond to the introduction.

"And you are Danielle Madison," he murmured. The ironic twist to the words made her aware that he was mocking her a little for not introducing herself in return.

"How do you know my name?"

"I must have heard it around somewhere," he replied, his expression bland.

She looked at him suspiciously. "I believe I'll take the stairs," she said, edging that way.

The elevator doors opened just as she finished speaking.

Agent Sexy—er, Teague McCauley, she corrected herself—stepped inside and held the doors for her. "Might as well ride now."

She thought about turning and hurrying toward the staircase.

But then she remembered that she didn't let any man intimidate her now. And besides, this guy was safe enough, she assured herself, stepping into the car and turning her back to him. He was her neighbor. An FBI agent. Nothing to worry about, as long as they kept their interactions fleeting and impersonal.

"Got big plans for the weekend?" he asked in the tone of someone making polite small talk.

She kept her eyes on the closed doors in front of her. "Not really."

"Me, either," he said, even though she hadn't asked. "I was thinking about going to a club or something tonight."

She knew he worked a lot, just from those casual observations of his activities. She doubted that he'd had a free Saturday night in the past month or more, since she'd occasionally seen him coming in late in the evenings looking as though he'd just put in a rough twelve or fourteen hours on the job. Certainly not giving the appearance that he'd been out clubbing or socializing.

Though she avoided clubs like the plague these days, she couldn't blame him for wanting an evening out on the town. He was youngish—early thirties, maybe? Only a few years older than herself. Certainly attractive. Looked healthy enough. He shouldn't have any trouble at all finding companionship for the night. It occurred to her only then that she'd never seen him bring anyone home with him. No one. Not that he was home that much, really, but she'd have thought he'd have a friend over. A date. Someone.

And then she realized that in the past year she'd lived in her apartment here, she'd rarely invited anyone inside, either. She hadn't made many friends since she'd moved to Little Rock. Didn't date very often, and usually chose not to extend those dates past her doorstep. Her apartment had become her refuge. Her sanctuary. Maybe Teague McCauley felt the same way about his place?

She wondered if this conversation was leading up to him asking her out. Maybe to join him for an evening in the clubs. If so, she hoped she would be able to politely decline without making it awkward when they ran into each other in the hallway from now on.

The elevator stopped on the third floor and she stepped out, bracing herself for him to try to delay her. Instead, he turned toward his own apartment without looking back, saying over his shoulder, "See you around."

"Um, yeah. See you." Suddenly aware that she was staring after him, she hurried to her own door, chagrined at her behavior.

Wouldn't her brother have laughed if he'd seen that exchange? She closed herself into her tidy, if inexpensively furnished living room with a frown of self-derision. She'd honestly thought Teague McCauley, aka Agent Sexy, had been angling to ask her out. She'd wasted several minutes mentally practicing polite rejections and it turned out he hadn't been interested after all. In fact, she thought he'd made it fairly clear that she didn't ever have to worry about that from him. Apparently, she wasn't his type.

Clay, her twenty-one-year-old brother, had often accused her of vanity. Of thinking she was "all that," as he had put it. And at the time he'd said it, he'd been right. That was back when she'd been a pampered daddy's girl. Before her doting father dropped dead just over three years ago of a heart attack at forty-five. And before Kurt Ritchie had taken away almost all of Dani's pride and self-respect.

God, she'd thought she was special. Pretty. Talented. Popular. Privileged.

What she had really been was spoiled. More needy than she'd realized. And so foolishly, dangerously gullible.

Maybe she'd been unknowingly slipping back into her old habits. Maybe the safe, ingratiating men she'd dated lately had made it easy to gravitate back into her old ways of thinking. If so, Teague McCauley had actually done her a favor with his lack of interest in her, she decided as she changed out of the blouse and slacks she had worn for work and into a comfortable pair of black yoga pants and a long-sleeved pink T-shirt.

Let him have his noisy clubs and eager women. She planned on a delightfully quiet evening with a good book, her favorite music and her own company. Which was exactly what she wanted, she assured herself firmly.

Someone tapped lightly on her door just as she headed for the kitchen in search of a light dinner. She froze, deciding immediately that Teague had come to ask her out after all. Maybe he'd just been giving her time to stew about his apparent indifference.

Very clever, she thought with a frown. If he thought playing hard to get was the way to pique her interest, he would just have to think again....

"Oh. Mrs. Parsons," she said, blinking at the little woman in the hallway outside her apartment. And didn't she feel like a fool for the second time in twenty minutes? "Is there something I can do for you?"

The petite, white-haired woman, whom Dani had always guessed to be somewhere in her early seventies, nodded. "I'm trying to rearrange some furniture and I wonder if you'd mind giving me a hand with my bookcase. It's a bit heavier than I thought."

Dani had helped her neighbor before, a time or two. Bringing in groceries. Reaching something on a shelf that was over the little woman's head. Changing a lightbulb. She never minded, figuring the woman asked as much out of loneliness as necessity. Mrs. Parsons had only one son, and he was a busy business owner who lived in Arizona, visiting only a couple of times a year. To her very vocal disappointment, he hadn't bothered to provide her with any grandchildren.

"I can try to help you, Mrs. Parsons, but if it's very heavy, we'll have to find someone else to help. The maintenance guy, maybe."

Mrs. Parsons nodded. "I think we can manage it. It's just a matter of getting it started in the right direction."

Still skeptical, having seen the woman's heavy furnishings, Dani followed her neighbor to the apartment next door.

Teague was rather pleased with himself when he walked across his living room an hour after he'd arrived home, headed again for the door. His hair was still wet from his shower, and he'd donned a plain white shirt and jeans, nothing fancy for tonight. He'd considered staying in once he'd gotten there, thinking an evening of crashing in front of the TV with a sandwich and a beer sounded pretty good after such a strenuous couple of months on the job. Instead, he'd talked himself into going to meet Mike. He'd gulped the sandwich, substituted soda for beer and then made himself change and shave for an evening out.

He was too young—and too sexually deprived—to keep living like some sort of workaholic monk. When riding an elevator with his uppity-but-good-looking neighbor was the high point of his social life, it was definitely time to do something drastic. He supposed hanging out with his friend in a singles' club, hoping to meet someone interested in a no-strings evening of fun, was better than nothing. Marginally.

Still, he couldn't help being amused by the way Dani had looked when he'd walked away from her in the hallway. He'd known very well that she'd more than half expected him to ask her to join him at the club he'd mentioned. When he hadn't asked—when he had, instead, walked away as if doing so had never even crossed his mind—she'd been more than a little piqued, despite her efforts not to let her reactions show.

Now *that* had been fun.

He suspected it was past time someone rattled the princess a little. Showed her not all men were eager lap puppies hoping for a crumb of attention from her.

He was just reaching for his keys when someone suddenly pounded on the other side of his door.

"Teague? Mr. McCauley? Are you there? We need your help!"

Dani, he thought immediately, all but leaping for the door. What the…?

She stood in the hallway, her dark-blue eyes wide, her long brown hair tumbled around her shoulders. "We need your help," she said.

And despite everything he had thought about her earlier, he merely nodded and followed as she turned to rush away.

Chapter Two

Rather than leading Teague to her apartment, as he had expected, Dani rushed to Mrs. Parsons's open door across the hall from him. Following, he stopped in the doorway, looking in amazement at the mess inside. "What on earth happened here?"

Wondering why he hadn't heard the crash—he must have still been in the shower when it happened—he scanned the room from the heavy bookcase lying facedown on the floor to the broken knick-knacks scattered across the carpet. A fragile-looking straight-backed chair had been knocked over when the bookcase fell, and books and magazines were tumbled all around.

Mrs. Parsons stood in the middle of the chaos, wringing her hands. "I can't even get to my bedroom," she said. "The bookcase is blocking the door."

"She wanted to move the bookcase a few inches to the left,"

Dani explained in a low voice. "I tried to tell her it was too heavy, but she just grabbed it and pulled."

"Was anyone hurt?"

"No, thank goodness," Mrs. Parsons said with a mixture of gratitude and sheepishness. "Dani pulled me out of the way just in time. I should have listened to her."

"If you could just help me lift the bookcase so she can get to her bedroom, I'll help her clean up the mess," Dani said to Teague. "She and I can't lift it by ourselves. We took everything off the shelves before we tried to move the case, but wouldn't you know we set them on the floor right where it fell. There's no telling what all is broken under there."

Relieved that they were unharmed, he nodded. "Mrs. Parsons, stand over there, where you won't be in any danger of being stepped on or bumped into. Dani and I can handle this."

"All right. I'll, um—I'll make coffee," she said, and bustled toward the kitchen before Teague could stop her.

"I'm sorry," Dani said with an apologetic expression. "I know you have plans for this evening, but it scared me so much when the bookcase fell. I thought for sure it would land on her. Then afterward, I couldn't think of anyone else to ask for help in lifting it."

"Not a problem," he assured her, kneeling to take one corner of the heavy oak case. "Can you handle that side? Just to keep it steady while I lift."

She nodded. "Right here?"

"Yeah. Lift with your knees. You don't want to hurt your back."

"I know."

The princess obviously didn't like being given instructions, even for her own good, he thought, judging by her rather curt tone.

With Teague doing most of the heavy lifting, they managed to set the case upright. "Where do you want it, Mrs. Parsons?" he asked. "I'll slide it into place for you."

"Right there," she said, coming back into the room to point to a position half a foot down the wall from where the case stood now. "Just far enough so I can set this chair beside it."

He placed his shoulder against the end of the bookcase and shoved, bracing the front with one hand so that there wouldn't be a repeat of the earlier catastrophe. "There?"

"Just a little more."

Seeing Dani's expression of sympathy, he smiled and pushed again.

"Right there," Mrs. Parsons said in satisfaction. "That's just right. Oh, dear, look at this mess."

"I hope nothing too valuable was broken," Teague said, reaching down to pick up a porcelain poodle that had been snapped neatly in half.

"Thank you, dear, but most of it is just stuff I've picked up here and there. Junk, really."

Noting the regret in her eyes when she picked up the pieces of a porcelain rose, he said gently, "It doesn't look like junk to me. I would guess these were things you treasured."

She blinked rapidly, then turned toward the kitchen. "The coffee should be ready. I'll pour. Just leave those things, Dani. I'll put everything in order later. Come have coffee. And I have snickerdoodles. I made them myself."

"I'd love to have coffee and cookies with you," Dani said, placing unbroken curios on the shelves of the bookcase. "But Mr. McCauley has plans for the evening."

"I always have time for cookies," Teague corrected her on an impulse, following the women into the kitchen. "And the name's Teague, by the way."

"Oh, this is nice." Mrs. Parsons beamed as she set a heaping serving plate on the table and pulled three mugs from a wooden mug tree. "I don't have company very often."

Thinking of the near disaster that had precipitated this impromptu visit, Teague felt a little guilty that he hadn't made more of an effort to speak to his obviously lonely neighbor when he passed her in the hallway. "I don't have homemade snickerdoodles very often," he said, putting two of the cinnamony cookies on the flowery dessert plate she'd set in front of him. "This is a real treat for me."

Dani had taken only one of the cookies for herself. She poured a drop of cream into her coffee. "I was just here last Monday, Mrs. Parsons," she reminded the older woman. "We had pecan pie when I helped you bring your groceries in, remember?"

"Oh, yes. We had a lovely visit, didn't we? I told you all about that nice young single man who goes to my church. You really should let me introduce you, Dani. I think you'd like him."

Looking a little embarrassed, Dani studiously avoided Teague's eyes. "Thank you, but as I told you then, I really don't have time to meet anyone new right now. Between work and classes, I have very little free time for socializing."

"Oh, you're too young to work all the time. That's what I was telling Hannah yesterday when she brought a package up for me. She's the young woman who moved in next door to you a few weeks ago, Teague. Have you met her yet?"

"No. I've seen her a couple of times, but we haven't introduced ourselves yet."

"She's a first-year medical student. All she does is study, study, study." Mrs. Parsons shook her head in disapproval. "She's only twenty-six and she keeps her head buried in those books. I told her she needed to take a little time to enjoy her youth while she has it, but she just smiled and said she would take time to enjoy life after she gets her degree. Just like you, Dani. You girls and your ambitions—there's more to life than careers, you know."

"What are you studying, Dani?" Teague asked.

She took a sip of her coffee, then set her mug down as she replied. "I'm taking music education classes at UALR. Minoring in psychology."

"Yeah? We have something in common. I have a business administration degree from UT, but I also minored in psych. Always thought it was really interesting."

"University of Texas?" Mrs. Parsons asked.

"Tennessee," he corrected her.

She shook her gray head in disapproval. "Oh, goodness. You're a Vol?"

He chuckled, remembering the red porcelain razorback figurine that had survived the crash in her living room. "Yes, ma'am. I guess you're a UA fan?"

"Oh, yes. I never miss watching the Razorbacks when they're on the TV. But I won't hold it against you," she assured him magnanimously.

He laughed. "I appreciate it."

He turned back to Dani. "You said you have a job in addition to taking classes. What do you do?"

"I teach piano lessons."

"She teaches six days a week," Mrs. Parsons expanded. "She has so many students that she's had to put some on a waiting list—and she's only been teaching here for a year."

"You must be very good," Teague murmured, studying Dani over the rim of his coffee mug.

Her left eyebrow rose a quarter of an inch. "I'm very good," she replied coolly.

He nearly choked on his coffee.

"The girls aren't the only ones who work all the time," Mrs. Parsons continued, apparently oblivious to any undercurrents between her guests. She pointed an arthritis-crooked finger at Teague. "Your hours are grueling. Doesn't the FBI allow its agents to get any rest?"

Forcing his attention away from Dani, he smiled at the older woman. "Rest hasn't been high on the priority list lately. But don't worry about that. I get enough."

"Make sure you do. Good looks and good health don't last forever, you know. You're lucky to have both. You should take better care of yourself."

Teague grinned and winked at Mrs. Parsons. "Thanks for the compliment—and the concern. I'll keep your advice in mind."

"You do that."

Having delivered her recommendations, Mrs. Parsons moved on to another subject. She chattered about a new shopping center being built not far from their building, about a new tenant on the second floor who had an unusual number of facial piercings, about a feature story she'd heard on the television morning show she'd watched earlier and about her son, who'd sent her roses last week for no reason.

The woman certainly could talk, Teague thought in amusement. He and Dani could hardly get a word in edgewise. Not that Dani seemed to be making much of an effort to do so. Was she always so quiet, or was his presence putting a damper on her conversation?

Dani didn't want to leave Mrs. Parsons to clean up her mess alone, but her neighbor seemed in no hurry to start picking up while Teague was there. In fact, Mrs. Parsons seemed to be enjoying having an attractive young man in her kitchen. If

Dani wasn't mistaken, the older woman was actually flirting a little, and Teague was lapping it up.

Hadn't he said he had plans to go clubbing that evening? Wouldn't he prefer flirting with women his own age rather than a giggling septuagenarian? Dani supposed it wasn't so late that he couldn't go to the club after leaving here, but he certainly seemed in no hurry to go.

Deciding she was going to have to take the initiative herself, she finally said, "I'll help you pick up in the living room now, Mrs. Parsons. I'm sure Teague has plans for this evening."

He shook his head. "Actually, I've decided to stay in for the rest of the evening. Maybe read or watch a little TV. I've had a long week, wouldn't mind a rest."

Dani frowned at him. "I thought you said you were meeting friends at a club."

He gave her a bland smile. "It wasn't a firm commitment. Just an option."

"I hope I haven't kept you away from your plans on a Saturday night," Mrs. Parsons fretted.

Turning a warm smile in her direction, he shook his head again. "Don't worry about it. I've enjoyed the cookies and the conversation. Let me help you clear your living room."

"Absolutely not," she insisted, including both of them in her refusal. "You've done enough. I'd like to take my time to go through everything and decide what I want to keep and what I need to throw away. I'll do that myself."

Though both protested, she ushered them out without listening to any further offers of assistance. "Good night," she said, smiling at them before closing the door politely in their faces, leaving them standing in the hallway, staring at each other.

"Well," Teague said, "that was interesting."

Dani couldn't help smiling. "I suppose. I'm sorry about your plans for the evening, though."

He shrugged. "I'm not. I was making myself go, anyway. It seems to bother other people more than it does me that I've been working more than playing lately."

Dani wrinkled her nose. "That sounds familiar."

It seemed like someone was always nagging at her about working too hard these days. Teague would probably identify with that, but he could never appreciate the true irony of the situation in her case. In all of her life prior to moving to Little Rock over a year earlier, Dani had never been described as being overly industrious.

He studied her face. "Piano lessons, huh? Like, to kids?"

"Mostly children," she agreed. "A few adults."

"Where do you teach?"

"I rent a small studio not far from here."

"How long until you get your degree from the university?"

"I'll have my undergraduate degree in May. Next year I'll start working toward my master's degree."

"And then what?"

Doubting that he was really all that interested in her future plans, she shrugged. "I'm sort of playing that by ear."

She had ideas, but she had no intention of discussing them with Teague. Especially not out in the hallway. She turned toward her apartment. "Thank you again for helping us with the bookcase. Good night."

"Dani."

She looked over her shoulder. "Yes?"

Was he going to ask her out now? If so, her answer would be the same despite the relatively pleasant hour they'd just spent together. He might pretend to be a mild-mannered, senior-citizen-helping, cookie-eating workaholic, but all her senses warned her that this lean, strong, inscrutable FBI agent was a lot more complicated than he tried to appear. And if there was one thing Dani did not need in her life right now, it was another complicated relationship.

"You should get some rest. You look tired."

"Um—" Once again, he'd managed to render her speechless, in addition to bruising the feminine ego she'd thought she'd gotten under control a long time ago. "I will," she managed to say after a momentary hesitation.

Looking entirely too pleased with himself, he nodded and moved toward his own door.

Dani and Teague ran into each other several more times during the next two weeks as October faded into November. There were times when Dani wondered if he deliberately made that happen, but she found that rather hard to believe. Her schedule was as erratic and unpredictable as his own, so he couldn't possibly know when she would be arriving or leaving. It was only coincidence that they saw each other more lately than they had in the past; after all, they lived only a few yards apart.

And it wasn't as if he was interested in pursuing her, anyway, she reminded herself wryly. He'd had plenty of opportunities to ask her out, if he'd wanted, and he had pointedly let them pass by.

They arrived home at the same time on a wet, cold, early evening. The parking lot was undergoing a week of repairs, so they had to park farther away from the building entrance than usual. Dani had just climbed out of her SUV, protected from the downpour by her roomy umbrella, when she saw Teague close his car door, no umbrella in his hand.

"Duck under," she called out to him, motioning with her free hand. "There's room for us both."

Grinning, he crowded beneath the umbrella, matching his steps to hers as they hurried toward their building. Standing water on the pavement splashed upward from their feet, drenching the bottoms of the jeans they both wore on this Saturday evening. Dani's shoes were soaked through to her feet; she envied Teague the waterproof hiking boots she noted that he wore.

They were both laughing when they stumbled into the entryway. Water dripped from the umbrella and the parts of themselves that hadn't been beneath it. Juggling her bag beneath her arm, Dani closed the umbrella, trying not to soak everything around her.

"Wow," Teague said, pushing a hand through his damp hair. "It's really coming down out there."

"And it's cold," she added, shivering. "My toes are freezing."

"You should have worn thicker shoes."

"You're right. I should have."

"Thanks for the shelter," he said, nodding toward the umbrella. "I was still damp from getting into my car at the office."

She shivered again. "No problem. I think I'm going to hurry upstairs, change into dry clothes and have a cup of hot chocolate to try to get warm. I'm cold all the way to the bone."

"Hot chocolate. With marshmallows?" he asked, his expression instantly wistful.

"Maybe."

"Sounds good. My mom used to make hot chocolate with marshmallows for me on cold, rainy afternoons."

Even though she knew full well she was being played, she gave in. Who'd have imagined this tough FBI agent would have perfected the art of puppy-dog eyes? "I suppose I could make two cups of hot chocolate—if you'd like one."

His face lit up. "I'd love a cup, if it's not too much trouble."

She hoped she wouldn't regret this moment of weakness. "Just give me time to change and it'll be ready."

He pressed the elevator button. "I'll save you the discomfort of climbing stairs in squishy shoes."

She chuckled when her shoes squished as she walked into the elevator. Wet footprints glistened on the tile floor behind her. "I appreciate it."

He leaned against the back of the elevator, his arms crossed over his chest. "You're in a good mood today."

"I guess."

"Any particular reason?"

She shrugged. "It's just been a good day."

"Glad to hear it."

The elevator opened on their floor and she sloshed out. "I'll see you in a few minutes," she said.

"I'm looking forward to it." He moved toward his apartment, adding over his shoulder, "It's been a long time since I've had hot chocolate."

Dani smiled wryly as she walked into her apartment, kicking off her wet shoes the moment she was inside. Trust Teague to make sure she didn't think it was her company he was anticipating so eagerly. It was the hot chocolate that excited him—with marshmallows, apparently.

Which reminded her, she hoped she had some, she thought, hurrying into her small kitchen. Fortunately, she did. She remembered now that she'd picked up a bag when she'd bought the ingredients for the hot chocolate. Figuring she wouldn't have much time before he arrived, she moved into her bedroom to change out of her damp clothes.

Tossing the shirt and jeans she'd worn into the hamper, she stood in bra and panties in front of her closet, her hand hovering over the hangers. It annoyed her to realize how long it was taking her to make a decision. Why was she acting as if she were dressing for a date? This was just an impromptu cup of cocoa with a neighbor, nothing more.

Donning an old pair of jeans and a rather baggy navy sweater, she slipped her feet into warm, fuzzy pink slippers and tied her hair up in a careless ponytail. She didn't think she could make the message any more clear that she was making no effort to attract him.

He tapped on her door just as she was preparing to pour the cocoa into two sturdy mugs. She opened the door to him, and noticed immediately that he looked as though he'd had a quick shower in the fifteen minutes since they'd separated. His hair had been damp before; it was even more so now, slicked back from his face in a style that actually looked good on him.

He hadn't shaved, and that, along with the sideburns he wore, gave him a rugged, tough look that made her heart skip. For a fleeting moment she wished she'd taken a bit more care with her own appearance. And then she shook her head in annoyance, pointing out to herself that he wore jeans, a gray T-shirt and sneakers, as casual as she was herself. She'd have looked ridiculous had she dressed up for this. Not to mention that she had no reason to want to primp for him.

Teague sniffed the air. "I smell hot chocolate."

She smiled in response to his eagerness. "It's in the kitchen. I was just about to add the marshmallows."

"I like lots of marshmallows."

"Then come add your own." She led him into the kitchen.

She couldn't help laughing as she watched Teague stack marshmallows in his cup. "You aren't going to be able to get to your drink."

"Watch me," he said with a grin, carrying the mug to the

table. "I don't suppose you have anything to eat to go with this? I skipped lunch, and I'm kind of hungry."

He didn't lack for nerve. She supposed that was a good thing for an FBI agent. "I could make you a sandwich."

"That would be great, if it isn't too much trouble."

"It's no trouble." She watched him for a moment before moving toward the fridge. "How can you possibly drink that without getting a marshmallow mustache?"

He chuckled. "Talent. This is really good, Dani. Tastes just like I remember my mom making."

She sipped her own as she pulled the makings for a turkey and Swiss sandwich from the fridge. "Is your mother still living?"

"No, she died when I was a kid. My dad remarried a few years later. He's gone now, too, but I've stayed in contact with my stepmother."

"Does she live in this area?"

He shook his head. "She's in a retirement community in Florida. I get out to see her a couple of times a year. What about you? Is your family around here?"

"No, they all live in Atlanta."

"I thought that was a Georgia accent I heard from you. Both your parents still living?"

Keeping her back to him, she swallowed hard. "My mother is. My dad died of a heart attack a few years ago."

He must have heard the pain that she still couldn't quite hide when she talked about her father.

"I'm sorry. It's hard to lose them, isn't it?"

Some people said that sort of thing almost routinely, not knowing what else to say. Because Teague had lost his parents, she took the quiet question the way he'd probably intended it. Literally. "Yes, very hard. Do you want mustard or mayo?"

"Mustard."

"Lettuce?"

"Yes, please. Do you have any brothers or sisters?"

"An older sister, newly married, no children yet, and a younger brother, a single college student. You?"

Chuckling at the concise efficiency of her reply, he shook his head. "No siblings."

She set the sandwich and a handful of baked chips in front of him, noticing that he'd almost emptied his cocoa mug already. "Do you want something else to go with this? Cola? Iced tea?"

"Tea sounds good. Aren't you eating?"

"Not right now. I had a late lunch with one of my piano students and her mother."

He swallowed a big bite of the sandwich. "It's good," he murmured. "Thank you."

Setting a glass of iced tea in front of him, she took a seat across the table, her cooling cocoa gripped loosely between her hands. "You're welcome."

"This is nice," he said, smiling companionably at her. "It's good to have friends in the building."

Friends. She was beginning to think that really was all he wanted from her. She had to admit that was a rather new concept for her. She wasn't even sure it was entirely feasible— but she couldn't help but be intrigued by the possibility.

So what did one talk about with a guy who only wanted to be friends? Searching her mind, she came up with, "How long have you worked for the FBI?"

"Almost eight years. I tried a few different jobs after college before sort of stumbling into this when I was twenty-five."

"And are you— I don't know what you call it. A special agent?"

He smiled patiently. "Yes. That's what we're called."

"So you track down bad guys and stuff?"

"Yeah. Something like that."

"Do you like it?"

He didn't seem to quite know how to answer what she had thought of as a simple question. "It's my job," he said after a pause. "I guess you could say it's pretty much who I am."

"So you aren't tired of it?"

"Not tired of it. Just plain tired, at times," he replied with a wry twist to his mouth. "The hours have been pretty long lately."

"I've noticed. Don't you get vacation time?"

"I have some built up. I'm thinking about taking some days off around the holidays this year. Maybe I'll go see my stepmother. I could use some beach time."

"Sounds nice. I'll be going home to Atlanta for Thanksgiving."

He cocked his head. "Do I detect a hint of reluctance?"

"Oh. You know. Family."

He smiled. "Even though I haven't had a lot of dealings with family, I've heard enough from others to understand what you mean."

"I'm sorry. I hope I didn't sound insensitive."

"No, you didn't. What's your family like?"

She laughed shortly. "That's a little hard to answer. Why do you ask?"

"Not having much of a family of my own, I guess I'm curious about other people's."

When he put it that way, it seemed churlish not to at least attempt a reply. "My grandmother is nosy, blunt-spoken, addicted to celebrity gossip and rabidly loyal when it comes to her friends and family. Mother's sort of flaky, has an incurable addiction to cutesy country decor and has a heart as big as Georgia. Rachel's a talented interior designer, the smart, capable, organized one in the family. She's married to a nice, good-looking physician, Mark Brannon.

"My brother, Clay, is still figuring out who and what he is. He came close to turning into a real loser a year or so ago, but Mark's been a good influence on him. Clay seems to be trying to make something of himself now. He's a decent guy, really, just drifted into the wrong crowd for a while."

"That happens." Popping the last chip into his mouth, Teague crunched, swallowed, washed it down with a sip of tea, then asked, "How would your family describe you, if I asked them?"

She grimaced. "Let's just say I'm working to change the way they would describe me."

He digested that with a thoughtful nod. "So, how'd you end up in Little Rock?"

"I needed a change of scenery." Which was all she intended to tell him about that. Her college scholarship, the money her grandmother had given her to fund the move and help her get set up in the piano-lesson business, the reasons she'd felt the need for that change of scenery—all of that was more than a casually friendly neighbor needed to know.

Something about the way he looked at her let her know he'd read a lot more than she'd intended into her nonanswer, but he let it go. He stood and carried his plate, glass and cocoa mug to the sink, where he rinsed and stacked them. "Thanks for the food," he said. "I needed the boost before I go out again."

"You're going out again tonight?" She tilted her head, listening to the rain still hammering against the windows. "In this?"

"No choice," he said with a shrug. "Working a case."

"At the risk of sounding like Mrs. Parsons, you really shouldn't work so hard."

He grinned and chucked her chin lightly with his knuckles. "Trust me, you look nothing like Mrs. Parsons."

Wondering how to take that, she followed him to the door. "So, should I advise you to be careful tonight?"

"Sure. It's always nice to have someone express concern."

"Okay, then I will. Be careful."

He paused in the doorway, one foot out in the hall. "Worried about me?"

She waved a hand in a negligent gesture. "You're a decent neighbor. Quiet. Handy with furniture crises. Since you never know what you're going to get with neighbors, I'd just as soon not have to deal with a new one."

He laughed. "Trust you to keep my ego in check."

Because that was so close to the things she'd thought about him, she laughed, too.

He took another step out. "See you around, Dani."

"Teague?" His name left her before she'd planned what she was going to ask.

"Yeah?"

Oh, what the heck. It was going to drive her nuts if she didn't get this cleared up. "You aren't going to ask me out, are you?"

His grin widened. "Nope."

"Not your type?"

He looked rather smugly delighted that she'd asked. "Too high maintenance."

Surprised, she lifted an eyebrow. "You think so?"

"Honey, I know so." He turned and strode down the hallway toward his door, saying over his shoulder, "Thanks again for the cocoa and the sandwich."

Rather bemused, Dani closed her door and turned the lock. After a moment she started to laugh.

Chapter Three

Dani met her newest neighbor a little more than a week later. They crashed into each other—literally—when Dani stepped out of her apartment just as Hannah Ross stumbled out of the elevator, her arms piled so high with books that she didn't even see Dani coming her way.

"I'm so sorry," Hannah said, her fair cheeks almost as red as the curly hair she'd pulled back into a low ponytail. "I wasn't paying attention. I hope you aren't hurt."

"No, I'm fine. Are you?" Dani bent to gather a couple of the thick textbooks scattered on the ugly green hallway carpet.

"Sure, I'm okay. I'm Hannah Ross, by the way."

"The medical student. I know. Mrs. Parsons told me."

Hannah smiled, her amber eyes lighting up. "She's a sweet woman, isn't she? She reminds me of my great-aunt."

"Yes, I've grown very fond of her. I'm Dani Madison, as she probably told you."

"Piano teacher and music student," Hannah murmured, proving that Mrs. Parsons had been chattering to her, too. "It's nice to officially meet you."

They'd nodded and exchanged greetings in the past, but this was the first time they'd bothered to introduce themselves. Dani had thought the other woman was shy, perhaps. Or maybe one of those women who took an unreasonable dislike to Dani on sight—as a few women had. Now she was back to the shy theory, since Hannah's smile looked friendly enough.

Dani, herself, had been so absorbed with work and studying that she hadn't really thought to make friends with her neighbors, other than Mrs. Parsons, who didn't really give anyone a choice about being her friend. Teague hadn't given her a lot of choice, either, she thought with a slight smile. She might as well get to know Hannah while she was at it.

"It's nice to meet you, too." Standing, she set the books she'd gathered on top of the pile in Hannah's arms. "Looks like you've got a long night ahead."

Hannah nodded gravely. "I have a gross-anatomy test next week. They're killers."

"I can imagine. My brother-in-law is a doctor, specializing in geriatrics. He's talked about how hard medical school is, especially that first year."

Hannah sighed. "They keep telling me it gets easier. I just hope I survive that long."

"You will. So, good luck on your test."

"Thanks. Um, maybe you want to get a pizza or something sometime? I've only lived in this city a couple of months and I haven't met many people my age yet. As for single guys— I don't think they exist around here."

Dani laughed. "They exist. It's just that the pickings seem pretty slim at times. And yeah, give me a call sometime when you're taking a break from studying and we'll order pizza and watch chick films."

Hannah smiled. "That sounds like fun. It'll give me incentive to keep studying for this test."

So now she had another potential friend in the building, Dani thought as she stepped into the elevator, tucking her big tote bag more snugly beneath her arm. An old woman, a frazzled med student and a sexy fed. A diverse group, that, and she didn't know which one was the more surprising as a friend.

As for which was the more disturbing—well, no question there. Only one of them had an uncomfortable habit of showing up unbidden in her daydreams.

Pushing that errant thought to the back of her mind, she moved to the back of the car when a young woman and her infant got on the elevator on the second floor. Nodding a greeting, she reflected on how her life had changed since she'd moved away from Georgia. She'd had dozens of friends there. An active social life. A growing reputation as a club singer. Family.

Now, with some distance behind her, she could see that former life a bit more clearly. Many of her friends had been of the fair-weather variety, hanging around only for the good times, notably absent during the bad. Her social life had consisted of a series of empty, unsatisfying relationships that had eventually led to a nearly disastrous affair with a man who'd almost destroyed her pride and self-esteem—and had once even resorted to physical violence. The clubs had been where she had met the string of losers and users she'd dated. And her family, while loving and well intentioned, had made it much too easy for her to continue her self-destructive ways by always bailing her out of trouble.

She had spent the past year trying to make a better life for herself. Pursuing a degree. Paying her own bills with money she made from her piano students, learning to deal with her own problems. Dating rarely, and then only on her own terms.

She didn't really miss the people she'd hung out with, since she had stayed in occasional contact with the real friends in the group. She missed singing in the clubs sometimes. Frankly, she had enjoyed the applause. Though she knew she had talent, she had never particularly craved a career in the entertainment business. And she still sang quite often in the music department at the university, but she made little effort to take any starring parts.

She had finally, belatedly arrived at the conclusion that she didn't need a spotlight to make her feel good about herself. Just as she didn't need a man's approval to validate her self-worth. She had been fortunate to figure that out at a relatively young age, and after only one painfully dysfunctional relationship. It took some women years to come to the same conclusion. Others, unfortunately, never got there, drifting from one bad situation to another, looking to others for something they could never seem to find within themselves.

And she was falling into psych-student-think, she realized with a grimace, climbing into her vehicle on her way to several scheduled piano lessons. It was typical of the average psychology student to either try to identify everyone around with some exotic neurosis, or to try to self-diagnose those same problems. Maybe she should just concentrate on her schedule for the rest of the day. Her life was on track now, and she intended to keep it that way.

Dani opened the back of her miniature SUV and studied the wooden rocking chair angled precariously inside. She'd barely been able to fit it in, and then only after several tries and assistance from a couple of helpful—and flirtatious—teenage boys. She smiled, remembering how cute they'd been with their swaggering and posturing, and then felt a bit old for thinking of them that way.

Reaching into her vehicle, she got a good grasp on the chair, preparing to haul it out.

"Hang on a minute." Teague spoke from right behind her. "Let me help you with that."

While she hadn't minded accepting help from the teenagers, doing so from Teague was a little different. "I can handle it."

"I'm sure you can, but you said I was handy with furniture, remember? When you listed the reasons why I made a pretty good neighbor. I don't want to risk my rep."

After a very brief mental debate, she stepped back, deciding that accepting his assistance with this relatively minor task was hardly admitting helplessness. "Thank you."

"You're welcome." He worked the chair carefully out of the SUV, taking pains to do no damage to either. "It almost didn't fit in there, huh?"

"It took some effort," she agreed.

"Nice chair."

"I bought it at a garage sale down the street. I love rocking chairs, and when I saw it sitting there, I had to stop."

"It's in really good shape. Looks comfortable."

"Yeah. I was lucky to spot it before someone else did. The lady I bought it from said she forgot to set it out earlier. It could stand to be refinished eventually, but I think it looks fine for now."

Carrying the chair toward the building entrance, Teague asked, "Do you shop at garage sales often?"

She shrugged, following him to the elevator. "I've found a

few bargains that way. I don't have a lot of extra money for decorating right now, so garage sales are a good resource."

"Your apartment looks nice. Wherever you shop, you choose nice things."

"Thanks." The offhanded compliment pleased her more than it should have. "My sister's the one with the decorating talent. Maybe I picked up a few tips from her along the way."

"Or maybe you have talent of your own," he suggested, hauling the rocker into the elevator.

She laughed when he set the chair down and took a seat as the elevator rose. "Comfy?"

"Mmm." He yawned and rocked slowly. "I could probably take a nap right here."

"You do look tired," she commented, studying the shadows beneath his closed eyes.

"Thanks a lot," he murmured without lifting his lids.

"I haven't seen you around for the past week."

"Been working out of town. Got back late last night."

He looked really good sitting in her rocker with his eyes closed, his jeaned legs stretched out in front of him, hands crossed on his stomach. She had to clear her throat silently before asking, "Where have you been?"

"Oh. You know. I could tell you, but then—"

She rolled her eyes. "You'd have to kill me," she said, completing the tired, overused joke.

"No. I was going to say, but then you'd have to pretend to be interested," he said, opening his eyes with a smart-aleck grin.

She laughed as the elevator doors opened. "So, when you're finished with your nap, would you mind bringing the chair to my place?"

He sighed heavily and lumbered to his feet, hoisting the rocking chair up again while she held the elevator doors open.

"Where do you want it?" he asked when she opened her apartment door.

"Just set it in that corner," she said, pointing. "I'll decide exactly where I want it later."

"No problem." He deposited the chair, then headed for the door. "See you later, Dani."

"Can I offer you a soft drink or anything before you go?" she asked. "As a thank-you for bringing up my chair?"

"I'll take a rain check, if you don't mind. I've got plans for tonight and I need to clean up first."

"Okay. Well…thank you."

He shot her a smile. "You're welcome."

He let himself out.

Dani sat in the rocking chair, stroking her hands down the worn-smooth maple arms. It was only her imagination, of course, that the seat was still warm from Teague sitting in it.

She wondered about his plans for the evening. Was he working again? Or socializing? Was he seeing someone? Someone he considered less "high maintenance" than her? Someone who could enjoy his company without worrying about getting too deeply involved, or losing herself in a one-sided relationship?

She released a long, slightly wistful sigh, then pushed herself to her feet. She had a small steak in the fridge. She'd bought it on sale yesterday, and she had planned a special dinner for herself tonight. The steak, a baked potato and a crisp salad—a real treat considering her limited food budget. A feast for one, of which she intended to savor every bite. Without once thinking about Teague.

Okay, so maybe the latter was improbable, she thought ruefully, opening the refrigerator door. But she'd try to enjoy her meal anyway.

* * *

"Great party, huh?"

Looking up from the single can of beer he'd been nursing for the past half hour, Teague nodded in response to Mike's shouted question. Then he leaned closer to his friend to ask, "Does it mean I'm getting old if I say that I wish they'd turn the music down a little?"

"Yeah. That's exactly what it means," Mike said with a laugh, leaning against the arched doorway that separated the living room from the formal dining room of the home in which the party was being held. The house was owned by Pete Schram, a lawyer who did some work for the FBI, and Pete's girlfriend, an up-and-coming fashion designer who answered only to the name of "Z." Z liked to entertain, and Pete indulged her by cohosting parties at least once a month. Teague had dropped in on a few, finding them always loud, frenetic, cheerful, exhausting. More so the latter tonight, since he was already tired, anyway.

He shouldn't have come, really. Not after the week he'd put in on the job. But he'd found himself contemplating an evening alone in front of the TV, followed by turning in early, and that had made him feel even older than his wish that someone would turn the music down. Besides, if he'd sat at home, he'd find himself thinking too much about Dani, which was a bad habit he'd gotten into lately. He really needed to spend some time with another woman.

"Hey, isn't that Kelly Something-or-other over there? The one you went out with a couple of times last spring?"

Looking in the direction of Mike's nod, Teague spotted the curvy blonde smiling back at him from the other side of the room. "Callie, not Kelly. And yeah, she and I have been out a few times."

Memorable times, he added silently. Callie's one goal in life was to have a good time, making sure everyone around her did, as well. He'd always had fun with Callie, but that had been the extent of their relationship. She had a well-known aversion to permanent commitments, and he hadn't been looking for anything more than someone to relax with between assignments. They had served each other's purposes quite well while they'd been together.

Maybe tonight was the time for them to reconnect. He had a couple days off, and she looked amenable. Callie would keep him too occupied for a few days to think about...well, anyone else.

Or would she? Sending her a smile in return, he turned slightly away, breaking the eye contact. No need to rush into anything this evening. Especially since he wasn't at all sure he wouldn't be thinking about someone else even if he was with Callie.

"So, aren't you going over there?" Mike prodded.

"I don't think so tonight. I'm just back from that mess in Texarkana. I'm thinking about going home and crashing."

"Oh, man." His friend studied his face with a frown. "You're thinking about *her*, aren't you? The princess."

It wasn't the first time Mike had brought Dani up since Teague had carelessly mentioned her that afternoon at the office. Mike seemed to think Teague was developing a thing for Dani, despite Teague's assurances that he wasn't that masochistic.

"I'm just tired," Teague argued. "Didn't you just agree that I'm getting older?"

"Not that old. And you haven't been acting quite right since that day I caught you grinning to yourself about something the princess said."

"Stop calling her that, okay?"

"You were the one who described her that way," Mike reminded him. "Hot, but high maintenance, I think you said. Have you changed your mind?"

After a momentary pause, Teague shrugged. "Well no, not exactly. But she's not so bad, really."

"Oh, yeah?"

Teague gave his friend a repressive frown. "This isn't junior high, Ferguson."

"And yet you're still standing here mooning over the hot girl. So the difference would be…?"

Teague made a suggestion that would have gotten his mouth washed out with soap, had his stepmother heard it. Mike merely laughed.

"Hey there, sexy. It's been a while."

Both men turned in response to the throaty drawl. Callie had strolled to their side of the room, accompanied by a tall, slender brunette who was eyeing Mike in blatant approval. Cleavage prominently displayed, Callie touched Teague's shoulder with a perfectly manicured hand. "So where have you been?"

"Oh. You know. Around."

She laughed huskily, and he remembered just how that laugh sounded in a dark, steamy room. "Yeah. Me, too. So, maybe we'll end up in the same place again sometime soon?"

"Yeah, maybe we will." He knew it would only take a word from him for that "sometime soon" to be that very night. If he'd had any sense at all, he'd have said that word right then, before she found someone else to have fun with that evening. But instead he made a lame excuse about wanting something to drink, and he wandered off to the bar, leaving Mike to entertain the women on his own.

* * *

Dani had just finished an assignment for a Monday-morning class when someone rapped on her door Sunday afternoon. Closing her notebook, she crossed the room and looked through the peephole, thinking her caller might be Mrs. Parsons.

Seeing Teague in the hallway instead elicited her usual reaction; she ran a quick hand through her hair and glanced down to check that her chocolate-colored top and khaki pants were reasonably neat. For some reason Teague always made her conscious of her appearance, though she'd tried to put less emphasis on that during the past year.

She opened the door. "Are you hungry again?"

He chuckled. "No. Bored."

"And what am I supposed to do about that?"

He gave her an enticing look similar to the one that had earned him a cup of hot chocolate and a sandwich just over a week earlier. "I thought maybe you'd like to go see a movie with me."

"Oh. I—"

"It's not a date," he assured her. "I won't be making any moves on you during the movie or afterward. I won't even buy you popcorn, if that makes you feel any better. I just hate going to movies by myself and all my other friends already have plans."

It was hardly the most flattering invitation she had ever received—and yet it had the result of making her feel relatively comfortable about accepting. If Teague really didn't see this as a date, or a preliminary to anything of the sort, then there was no real reason she should turn him down, right? If her own imagination got away with her during the evening— well, that was a problem she would deal with at the time.

"Okay," she said, because she could use a couple of hours of relaxation herself. "What movie do you want to see?"

He looked both pleased and a bit surprised that she'd accepted so easily.

"Just as friends," she reminded him.

Holding up a hand in an I-swear gesture, he nodded. "I hope you like action movies. I don't do tear-jerkers."

"Neither do I. Give me an action movie any day."

His smile widened. "My kind of friend. How does the latest superhero film sound to you?"

"From what I've heard, it's got enough eye candy to keep us both entertained. Let me get my bag."

She heard him chuckle as she turned away, and if there was a hint of smugness in the sound, she chose to ignore it.

Chapter Four

"Wow. I hope I never do anything to annoy you."

Snapping his seat belt, Teague looked at Dani in surprise. "Why do you say that?"

Strapped into her own seat, she exaggerated a shiver. "The look you gave that woman over the back of your seat. I could almost feel the cold waves coming off you. It's no wonder she got up and nearly fell over herself trying to move to another part of the theater."

"She was kicking my seat. And text messaging through the first ten minutes of the movie. All that beeping wasn't driving you crazy?"

"Well, yes. And she was kicking my seat, too. I'm glad you got her to move. I'm just impressed that you did so without saying a word. All you had to do was turn and look at her and she bolted. Do they teach you that glower in FBI training?"

He laughed and shrugged. "I don't know what you're talking about. I just glared at her the same way anyone else would. She got the message that she was annoying us, so she moved. Which made it much easier to concentrate on the movie after that—not that there was much plot to keep up with," he added wryly.

"No. But it was entertaining, anyway," she agreed. She didn't bother to argue with his assertion that he didn't look any more dangerous than anyone else. But he was wrong. As charming and friendly as Teague could be, when he turned serious, there was a definite air of danger around him.

They talked about the movie for a couple more minutes, and then Teague asked, "Are you hungry? Because I could go for a burger."

"Yeah, sure. A burger sounds good."

He chose a locally owned restaurant that he swore made the best burgers in town. Since she'd never eaten there, she told him she would judge that after she'd had one.

"I like the pepper jack burger, myself," he advised as they slid into a booth. "With seasoned fries on the side."

"Hey, Teague." A chubby bottle-blonde set a large glass of iced tea in front of him with a flirty smile. "Where've you been?"

"Around. You're looking good, Annie."

She patted his cheek. "Sweet talker. What can I get you to drink, hon?"

Realizing the server was talking to her now, Dani replied, "I'll have the tea, thank you."

"Coming right up." Leaving a menu with Dani, Annie sashayed away.

Dani looked at the selection of burgers and other casual food on the laminated menu. "Not a lot of low-cal options here."

"No. That's not why people come here. Everyone deserves to be bad every once in a while, don't you think?"

She wondered if he was only talking about food, then decided she was trying too hard to read between his lines. "I suppose so. I'll have the mushroom Swiss burger."

"Good choice. The onion rings are superb here. They make them with sweet onions and serve them with ranch dip."

Sighing as she thought of how many salads she was going to have to eat to make up for this meal, Dani said, "Then I'll have to order them."

"Good. You can have some of my fries and I'll take some of your rings. That way we get the best of both."

Setting the menu aside, she nodded. "Sounds like a plan."

She was actually having a good time, she decided as they chatted a bit more about the lightweight film, of which the special effects had been the only particularly notable feature. It was nice being out with a man who seemed to want nothing from her but companionship. Friendship.

She was under no pressure to try to impress him or please him. If, for some reason, he decided not to ask her to join him for another outing, she wouldn't have to interpret it to mean that something was lacking in her.

She wouldn't date him, because he was just the kind of man who just might make her return to those unhealthy habits—but she could be his friend. She was taking a bit of a risk in letting him get even that close.

Since she couldn't deny the attraction she felt for him, she would have to be very careful.

No problem, she assured herself, and then crossed her fingers beneath the table.

During the next few days, Teague came to some very interesting conclusions about Dani. Her trust issues went even deeper than he had originally realized, and he had an uncomfortable suspicion that her wariness was based on experience. Had some jerk hurt her...? Physically, in addition to emotionally?

She'd told him once in passing that she'd taken six months of self-defense classes when she'd first moved to the area, stopping only when her schedule had gotten too hectic. Even that fit into the pattern of a woman who had learned the hard way that she had to prepare to defend herself.

That would explain her preference now for dating men she could so easily control, he mused. And the way she got all prickly when it seemed that anyone was getting a bit too bossy, the way she had when he had made a comment one evening in the elevator that she should be careful when coming in by herself late at night. She had informed him in no uncertain terms that she was fully capable of watching out for herself.

They had been together a couple more times since their movie outing. Once to share a pizza and watch a football game on TV. Another time to play a board game with Mrs. Parsons, who had been so pleased at having company that she'd giggled like a schoolgirl all evening.

He and Dani talked quite easily, now that he'd convinced her he thought of her only as a friend. Their conversation consisted mostly of small talk and teasing. He kidded her about being high maintenance and dating guys she could lead around by the nose—to which she cheerfully admitted. She ribbed him about his job as an agent and made good-natured "007" jokes at his expense.

Anytime the subject got a bit too close to her past relationships, she cut him off abruptly. She asked very few questions about his own past, maybe so as not to encourage him to inquire about hers.

He tapped on her door on a Wednesday afternoon a couple

of weeks before Thanksgiving. She opened it with a distracted expression that, along with her ultracasual sweatshirt and grubby jeans, told him she'd been studying.

"Test tomorrow?" he asked, recognizing the look by now.

She nodded. "Big one."

"I won't keep you, then. I just wanted to give you this."

She lifted her eyebrows in question when he pressed a brown paper bag into her hand. "What is it?"

"Two bananas and a pear."

She laughed in surprise. "Um…okay. So, why?"

"Because I'm going to be extremely busy for the next few weeks and I'm not sure I'll be home to eat them before they go bad. I'd hate to see them go to waste."

"Trust me," she said. "They won't go to waste."

"Good. I hope you enjoy them."

"You want to come in for a few minutes? I can make hot chocolate."

He shook his head with regret. "As tempting as that sounds, I have to pass. I've got to work tonight."

"Work? That's what you're going to be doing for the next few weeks? I thought maybe you were finally getting away for that vacation you've been talking about taking."

"I wish," he muttered, thinking of the unsavory assignment he was about to dive into.

She searched his face, then spoke lightly, "Do I have to warn you again to be careful?"

"Probably not a bad idea."

"Then I will," she said, her smile just a little strained now. "Be careful, okay? I don't have that many friends around here."

"How about a friendly kiss on the cheek? For luck?"

She shook a finger at him, but then placed a soft kiss on the cheek he offered hopefully. Her lips were as warm and inviting as he'd always imagined them to be. It was all he could do not to turn his head just that couple of inches required to make their mouths meet. Instead he managed a casual smile when she drew back. "That ought to do it. Thanks."

Her cheeks were just a bit pink when she said somewhat gruffly, "Just take care of yourself, okay? I'll give you a rain check on that cup of hot chocolate."

"I'll take you up on that," he promised. "See you, Dani."

He was aware that she watched him walk away for a few moments before she closed her door. He hoped it wasn't too obvious how hard it was for him to leave her.

They were making pretty good progress in getting closer. He wouldn't want to scare her off now.

Dani was rather surprised, and a bit dismayed, by how much she missed Teague during the next couple of weeks. She found herself looking almost constantly toward his apartment door, wondering how he was, when he would be back, whether he was in any danger.

He probably was, she thought somberly. His was not a safe, sedate career. She could tell when he'd told her he'd be gone for a while that it wasn't an assignment he was looking forward to. She'd learned to read him at least that well.

Mrs. Parsons left a week before Thanksgiving for a long visit with her son in Arizona. She would return the first week of January. She had confided in Dani that she was excited about the trip, but a bit nervous, as well.

It would be the longest period she had spent with her son and his wife, and she hoped they would all get along well. She suspected that her son would use the opportunity to try to convince her to move there permanently to be closer to him, and she wasn't sure how she felt about leaving the state where she'd resided for more than fifty years. She had lived in her apartment since her husband had died five years earlier, and she was comfortable there, content for the most part. She didn't know if she would like living in Arizona.

Dani reminded her that this visit would be a good time for all of Mrs. Parsons's family to decide if they wanted to live that close together. "You're a competent adult," she had reminded the older woman. "Ultimately, it's your choice whether you move there or stay here."

Looking reassured, Mrs. Parsons departed for her vacation, leaving a quiet apartment wing behind her, since Hannah was taking tests and rarely surfaced from her studies. Which made Dani miss Teague all the more.

Her sister, Rachel, called on Friday, the day after Mrs. Parsons left. "You're still coming for Thanksgiving, right?"

"Of course I'm still coming," Dani replied with mild exasperation. "Why wouldn't I?"

"You did cancel out the last time you said you'd come home," Rachel reminded her.

"I told you, I had a big assignment I had to finish and I couldn't get away that week. I'll be home next week. And again for Christmas, for that matter."

"Good. We miss you."

"I miss you, too."

"Enough to move back home? You can always finish your degree here."

"Don't start, Rachel. I like it here. Things are going well for me here. As much as I love you all, I need to be here, on my own, for a while. I'm not saying I'll never move back to Georgia, but for now this is where I need to be."

Rachel, who had never lived more than an hour's drive from the house where she and her siblings had grown up, sighed lightly through the phone lines. "I was pretty sure you'd say that, but it was worth a shot. So, how are your classes going?"

"I have all A's, if I can just keep it that way through finals next month."

"I'm sure you will. And I'm proud of you. Are your piano lessons still going well?"

"I have as many students as I can take right now. A waiting list for more. Several area teachers have retired lately, and I've been getting their 'orphaned' students. I have a few who are really talented. And even more who couldn't find a tune if I personally placed their fingers on the keys."

Rachel laughed. "Now you sound like Mrs. McNeal. She said very similar things about me, as I recall."

"You weren't that bad. You just preferred art and decorating to playing piano. Mother had to force you to practice."

"She tried. For ten years, until I finally refused to take any more lessons. You were always the one with the real musical talent. Do you ever sing solos anymore?"

"Only in the shower." Dani quickly changed the subject. "How's Mark?"

"He's great. We're driving to Alabama the day after Thanksgiving to spend the weekend with his family. Everyone's going to be there. Speaking of which, have you seen Joel and Nic lately?"

Rachel's pediatrician brother-in-law, Joel Brannon, and his police officer wife, Nic, lived less than an hour's drive from Dani's apartment building. Dani and Nic had gotten along very well during Rachel and Mark's wedding festivities, slipping away from the family chaos a couple of times to sip coffee and talk. It was during one of those chats that Dani had confided her intention to move away from her hometown for a fresh start. Nic had suggested that Dani look into the university at Little Rock, and here she had landed.

"I had dinner with them a couple of weeks ago. It's really funny seeing Nic pregnant. All tough and radiant at the same time."

"I can't wait to see her next week. How's everything else going with you? Have you made any new friends?"

Dani suspected that her sister was really asking if she was dating anyone. Rachel had expressed concern that Dani would let her painful experience with Kurt destroy her trust in all men. She'd spoken from experience, since Rachel had survived a couple of bad relationships herself, including a divorce, before she'd met and fallen in love with Mark.

She wouldn't say she'd been soured on all men, Dani thought solemnly. She knew there were plenty of decent guys out there. She knew quite a few of them. She just no longer trusted her own instincts about telling the good ones from the bad.

"I've gotten to know some of my neighbors," she said lightly. "An older woman, Mrs. Parsons, who reminds me a little of Grandma. And Teague, an FBI agent, and Hannah, a first-year med student. She lives directly across the hall from me. She seems nice, if a bit overwhelmed by her studies. It seems that I'm destined to be surrounded by doctors, doesn't it?"

Typically, Rachel zeroed in on the one significant name amid all the babbling. "Tell me about the FBI agent. Teague, you said?"

"Mmm. Seems like a nice enough guy, but he's gone a lot. Apparently FBI agents put in some pretty long hours."

"Is he cute?"

"Why do you ask?"

"He sounds cute. The way you talk about him, I mean."

Dani sighed in exasperation. "I've barely mentioned him."

"Mmm."

"If you're testing me to see if I really have learned to take care of myself without having a man in my life, you can rest assured that I've got an A in that subject, too," Dani said flatly. "I'm not involved with anyone, and I don't intend to be anytime soon. So let's leave it at that, shall we?"

"I wasn't trying to… I'm sorry, Dani, I was only teasing."

So maybe Dani had overreacted a little. She did that sometimes when she was reminded of the woman she used to be. "Sorry. Long day. I'll see you next week, okay? I'm really looking forward to the visit."

"So am I."

It had been the truth, Dani assured herself when she hung up the phone a few minutes later. She was looking forward to seeing her family again after several months of separation. And yet, a part of her was as nervous as Mrs. Parsons had been about her long visit with her son. Though it might have been foolish, she couldn't help worrying that being home again would set her back in her efforts to move forward with her life. To put the past behind her and become the new, improved Dani Madison.

But she wouldn't worry about that now, she vowed, reaching for her laptop and the stack of textbooks next to it. Somehow she would figure out a way to convince her family—and anyone else she might run into back home—that she was not the same person who had moved away all those months ago.

She dreamed of Teague that night. And when she woke, flushed and vaguely aroused, she realized that her subconscious was paying little attention to her efforts to keep her attraction to him under control.

Okay, she thought, splashing cold water onto her face. So

she was only human. And she hadn't let any man get too close to her in more than a year. It was only natural that she would be intrigued by the good-looking agent down the hall.

A little fantasizing never hurt anyone, she assured herself. The only real danger was in trying to turn fantasy into reality.

"Okay, Samantha, play it through one more time and then you can be done for today."

The seven-year-old girl on the piano bench next to Dani's chair protested with a whine. "Do I have to play it again?"

"Samantha, do what Ms. Madison says," the child's mother chided from a small couch on the opposite wall of the small studio.

Heaving a huge, long-suffering sigh, Samantha placed her fingers on the piano keyboard and lumbered discordantly through a first-year-student tune called "Playful Puppy." Dani thought that had there actually been a dog in the room, it would have been covering its ears with its paws and howling in pain. She almost wished she had that option herself.

"Very good, Samantha," she said with a big smile when the piano went mercifully silent. "Now, I know Thanksgiving is only three days away, but you be sure to practice when you can this week, okay? Your mommy will continue to put a star on your chart every time you practice, and when you have ten stars, I'll give you another sticker for your sticker book."

"I already have five stars," Samantha informed her.

"Very good. Then you're already halfway there." Dani wondered how Samantha kept accumulating practice stars without actually making any improvement in her playing. She had a sneaky suspicion that Mommy was being a bit generous with the star awarding. "Practice hard, okay? We have a lot of fun songs to play once you've mastered this one."

Which might be about the same time the kid got her driver's license, she added silently.

Samantha's mother wore an anxious smile that showed she was aware that her daughter wasn't exactly a piano prodigy. "Maybe she didn't practice quite as long as she should have," she confided, just a hint of defensiveness in her voice. "But she's so busy with her dance classes and soccer games and riding lessons, not to mention all the birthday parties she gets invited to attend. It's hard to find the time for everything."

"I understand," Dani replied sympathetically. "That's a busy schedule for a seven-year-old. You may have to choose a couple of activities that she enjoys the most and drop the others for a while."

"She just enjoys everything so much," the doting mother fretted. "I hate for her to miss out on anything."

Since Dani suspected that Samantha would be perfectly happy missing out on piano lessons, and was taking them only because her mother insisted, she merely nodded and showed the couple out. She made a mental note to give the child another month or so to display any enthusiasm at all for piano, and after that she would talk more seriously with the mother about making some decisions.

Sighing lightly, she packed her teaching materials into the big canvas tote she always carried and locked the little studio she rented by the month. She had canceled her lessons for the remainder of this holiday week, so she wouldn't be back for a whole seven days. She needed the break.

Located in an old school building, the studio was one of several rented by local music teachers. As she left the building, she could hear other pianos playing, in addition to guitars, wind instruments, a banjo and—she winced—either a whole bunch of cats fighting or a group of first-year violin students trying to play a tune in unison.

Okay, so it wasn't the private music school she wanted to someday own and operate, she thought, climbing into her SUV. What she made on her part-time lessons after paying rent here was just enough to pay her bills, and that was living frugally. But she enjoyed most of her students, and she was pursuing the degree that would give her an advantage if she did someday open her own music school. So it wasn't so bad.

Best of all, she was making her own way, on her own terms. She hadn't asked Rachel, or anyone else, for any favors or advice since she'd moved here. There had been a time, she thought with a wry glance at her silent cell phone, when she had called her sister at least twice a day with requests—no, more like demands—for Rachel's assistance with one thing or another.

She stopped by the grocery store on the way home, buying just enough to make a few relatively healthy meals-for-one for a couple of days. She would be leaving for Atlanta Wednesday, so she didn't need much.

The store was crowded for early on a Monday evening; she assumed people were already shopping for their Thanksgiving meals. She needed a few things at "Ubiquitous Mart," as she called the massive discount chain, but that could wait. She was getting tired, hungry, and she had a paper to write that was due in class the next day.

It was dark by the time she finally parked in her spot. That realization made her think of Teague, and his annoying warnings about being cautious after dark, as if she weren't smart enough to take care of herself. The parking lot was well lit, and she'd never felt uncomfortable, even coming in late. She couldn't afford an apartment complex with security or gated entrances, but she'd done her research and had chosen a building in a safe location and with an excellent safety record. Besides, if an FBI agent had chosen to live here, it must be reputable enough. She had never seen even one shady character lurking around.

The direction her thoughts had taken must have made her antsy. She found herself looking around as she juggled her tote bag and groceries to use her key card in the outer door. It was a bit unusual, but not entirely unprecedented, that no one else was in sight. Sometimes she just happened to come home when everyone else was having dinner or watching TV or something.

The elevator was empty. She checked carefully before stepping inside, just to be sure. The hallway was also vacant when she stepped out, and that was no surprise, either, since Mrs. Parsons was out of state, Hannah probably had her head buried in her textbooks and Teague was…heaven only knew where.

She carried her things into her apartment, dumped everything on her kitchen table and then realized she had left her purse in her car.

"Damn it," she muttered, her shoulders sagging with weariness as she considered leaving the purse where it was until morning.

She straightened with a sigh of resignation. She had to go back down. Leaving the purse in the car was just begging for a break-in, and she didn't want to go through the hassle of replacing her driver's license and credit cards. Not to mention the cash. Forty-five dollars. That was a lot to her these days.

Carrying her keys in her left hand, she crossed her living room and stepped out into the hallway again. She glanced at the stairwell, told herself she really could use the exercise, then pushed the elevator button anyway. Apparently, she was still feeling edgy. The thought of going down that empty stair-well alone made her a bit nervous.

She shook her head as she listened to the elevator rumbling up toward her. She really was in a strange mood tonight. She blamed it on Teague, she thought with a half smile. Even when he wasn't here, he made her jumpy.

The elevator doors slid open and she moved forward, auto-matically assuming it was as empty as the rest of the building had seemed that evening. She stopped with a gasp when a large, male figure stumbled out. Instinctively, she tried to move out of the way, dodging with one of the moves she'd learned in her self-defense classes. And then he grabbed her.

She drew a deep breath to scream, hoping there would be at least someone in the building to hear her. Her attacker fell heavily against her…and then began to slide downward. Still poised to run, she glanced down at him, then choked when she recognized him. Not that it was easy to do, with all the blood and bruises covering his face.

"Teague?"

He was on his knees now, and she fell to hers beside him, studying his battered face in horror. "Teague!"

His only response was a groan before he collapsed to the floor.

Chapter Five

Dani's first response to Teague's collapse was panic. She reached for her cell phone, then muttered a curse when she realized it was in her purse, still locked in her car. They needed a doctor, she thought. Quickly.

Glancing up, she jumped to her feet and pounded on the closest door. "Hannah! Are you in there? I need help."

After a moment the door flew open. Hannah peered out anxiously. "Dani? What's— Oh my God."

"He's hurt," Dani said unnecessarily, since Hannah had already seen Teague lying there. "Can you help him while I call an ambulance?"

"Me? Uh—"

"You're a medical student, aren't you?"

Her amber eyes huge in her suddenly pale face, Hannah shook her head frantically. "I'm a first-year medical student. We haven't actually seen patients yet, only simulated situations. Pretty much all I've learned so far is how to take blood pressure, listen to lungs and do a breast exam."

"Then I'll sit with him while you call an ambulance."

"No." With an obvious effort, Teague lifted himself onto one forearm. Dani hadn't even realized he was conscious. "No ambulance. And no breast exam, either," he added with a sickly smile for Hannah.

Dani hurried back to him when he made a move to stand. "What are you doing? Lie back down and let us—"

"No. I'm okay. Help me up."

"She's right, you know," Hannah said, even as she moved to his other side. "You should let us call someone. Or at least let us drive you to the emergency room."

"No." There was no mistaking the resolve in his voice as he pushed himself to his feet with their help. "I have a pathological aversion to hospitals. Just help me to my apartment and I'll see my own doctor tomorrow, if necessary."

"You're just going to lie in your apartment alone until you wake up in the morning—*if* you wake up in the morning," Dani summed up in exasperation.

"I'll be fine. I've been beaten up before. I know what to do."

Beaten up. The words made her stomach clench. But she would wait until later to ask about details. "Help me get him into my apartment," she said to Hannah. "I'll nag him about seeing a doctor after I make sure he's not going to pass out again."

"I didn't pass out," he muttered, swaying on his feet. "And I'll be fine in my own apartment."

"Can you get there without assistance? And get your key into the lock on the first try?" Dani demanded.

He looked toward his doorway, and she suspected it was swimming in front of his swollen, bruised eyes. "Uh—"

"Yeah, that's what I thought." She looked at Hannah again. "My place."

It was an indication of how much pain Teague was in that he didn't try to argue further.

Propping him up on either side, Dani and Hannah got him into Dani's living room and onto her couch.

"I have a first-aid kit," Dani said, moving toward the bathroom. "Watch him until I get back."

Hannah looked at Teague, who was resting his head against the back cushion, as if she wasn't at all sure what she was supposed to be watching for, but she nodded. "Okay."

Dani returned a few minutes later carrying the first-aid kit and a damp washcloth. "You haven't treated any patients?" she asked Hannah, who was sitting now by Teague, patting his pain-clenched fist.

Scooting away from Teague, Hannah shook her head. "Sorry. The first year is almost all class and lab work. We have standardized patients occasionally—actors who let us do simple exams on them—but I won't see real patients until my third year."

"I can wait," Teague muttered without opening his eyes.

"No, you can't," Dani answered repressively. "And this is no time to be kidding around. Your face is a mess. Heaven knows what the rest of you looks like."

"I'll let you see—if you and Hannah return the favor."

Hannah giggled.

Dani sighed. "Just shut up and let me clean your face."

"Yes, ma'am."

Standing, Hannah offered, "I'll run over to my apartment and make some chamomile tea. My granny swore it would cure anything from the common cold to broken bones."

"My mother believes the same thing," Dani murmured,

smoothing the washcloth over Teague's bloody face. "I have some in my kitchen."

"I know where everything is in mine," Hannah replied, moving toward the door. "And I left something in the oven I need to check."

Left alone with Teague, Dani concentrated on his injuries. Most of the blood seemed to have come from a cut on his forehead, just above his left eye. The eye itself was bruised and swollen, as were his cheek and chin. His nose had bled; it looked as though he had wiped it with the sleeve of his torn, dirty, long-sleeved black pullover. There were other bruises and small cuts on the right side of his face, though he'd escaped a black eye on that side.

He winced when he drew a deep breath. Broken ribs? Cracked, at least. She didn't know if he had a concussion, or any other broken bones. Internal injuries? There was no way to tell without a professional examination.

"You have to let me take you to a doctor."

"No. I'll see someone tomorrow."

"You don't need to wait until tomorrow. You need someone now. Please, Teague, let me—"

He lifted his eyelids to look her firmly in the eyes. "Dani. I've told you. I don't want to see a doctor right now. Trust me, I don't have a death wish. If I thought there was any need, I would go. But I'm going to be okay. It's mostly superficial."

"You probably have a broken rib."

"Probably a couple of cracked ones," he agreed, "but I can tape them up. I've done so before."

"You could be bleeding inside. You could have a concussion."

"I'm not bleeding inside. I've likely got a mild concussion, and my left ankle is twisted. I don't think it's broken. I can wrap that, too."

"Why are you so determined not to go to the emergency room?" she asked, genuinely confused.

He hesitated and then confessed, "I did something really stupid. Made a dumb error in judgment that got me beaten up by some gang members I was investigating. A couple of my associates showed up and helped me get them into custody, and I sort of downplayed how bad I was hurt until I managed to get away. I don't want an official report made. I'll take some of the vacation time I've got accumulated next week, after which I'll be recovered enough to go back to work. So no big deal."

It must have taken every ounce of strength he'd had to bluff his way through the arrest, she realized, noting that there was absolutely no color in his face now that wasn't either a bruise or a spot of dried blood. "You drove yourself home?"

He shook his head. "My buddy dropped me off. Another drove my car. I told them I could make it up to my apartment by myself."

"And then you collapsed off the elevator," she finished with a disapproving shake of her head. "They should have taken you to the E.R., even if you argued with them."

"I told you, they're my friends. I'd have done the same for them."

"Stupid, stubborn men," she grumbled beneath her breath.

He smiled and closed his eyes again. "Whatever."

She did the best she could with antibiotic ointment and plastic bandage strips, making him hold a bag of frozen peas to the left side of his face. Hannah returned with a ceramic teapot; Dani fetched three cups and they all had some, since Hannah asserted that they could probably all benefit from the soothing properties of the chamomile tea.

Dani noted that Hannah searched Teague's face almost constantly. Hannah might claim that she was only into the bookwork part of becoming a doctor, but she was obviously itching to do something to help him. Dani had noticed that same look on her brother-in-law's face when he'd seen someone in pain.

"That was really good, Hannah, thank you," Teague said after drinking about half his tea. He set the cup on a coaster, making a visible effort not to wince with the movement. Failing.

"I should go back to studying," she said, hovering beside the couch. "I still agree with Dani, though, Teague. I think you should probably see a doctor tonight."

"I appreciate your concern," he replied gently. "You'll make a great doctor. One I wouldn't hesitate to call upon— and that's saying something, because I don't like many doctors, on the whole."

She grimaced. "You're assuming I'll survive gross anatomy and genetics, of course."

"You will."

Dani walked Hannah to the door, where they both glanced back at Teague, who was lying back with his eyes closed again.

"He really shouldn't be alone tonight," Hannah said in a low voice.

"He won't be. I'll make him stay here so I can wake him up every so often."

"If he starts acting really disoriented or something, call me, whatever time it is. We'll get him to the E.R. if we have to hogtie him, okay?"

"It's a deal."

"I heard all that, you know," Teague said when Dani closed the door behind Hannah. He hadn't moved, nor opened his eyes, and she hadn't even been sure he was still awake. "I'll be fine in my own apartment. I'll set the alarm to wake me every couple of hours."

"The alarm can't take you to the hospital if you don't wake up," she retorted. "You'll stay here. My couch is pretty comfortable."

"Your bed's pretty big. I can see it from here through the open bedroom doorway. It would probably hold both of us."

"I know what you're doing." She wagged a finger at him. "You're trying to make me uncomfortable so I'll send you home and stop nagging you to go to the doctor. It's not going to work."

She drew a deep breath. "Now, you can tell me this is none of my business and that you're an adult who doesn't have to do anything I tell you to do. And you'd be right, of course. But you're the one who was determined to be my friend. And friends don't let friends do stupid, life-threatening things."

He opened his eyes to glittering slits—probably as far as he could open them at that moment. "Friends, huh?"

"Friends. *Just* friends. Which is why you're sleeping on the couch."

He chuckled quietly, closing his eyes again.

He looked so battered and tired that Dani felt her heart twist, despite the firm tone she'd been taking with him. She suspected much of that had been bluff, to keep herself from falling apart. Drawing another bracing breath, she asked quietly, "Have you had anything to eat?"

"I'm not really hungry. But you go ahead."

It was just past 6:00 p.m., but she could tell he was about ready to crash. "Why don't you go lie down on the bed while I make some dinner? I have some work to do this evening. I'll come in and check on you regularly."

He hesitated a moment before saying, "I need a shower. And clean clothes. I'm filthy. I'll just go to my place and…"

"I'll go get you some clean clothes. You can take a shower

here, when I get back. Please, Teague," she added quietly, when he looked prepared to argue again. "I'm worried about you."

Looking into her eyes, he sighed and surrendered. "Fine."

He dug in his pocket for his key. Tossing it to her, he told her where she could find his clothes and the stretch bandages he kept on hand for times like this. Feeling a mixture of concern and disapproval, she nodded.

"Dani—" he said when she turned to leave.

She paused at the door, looking back at him. "Is there something else you need?"

"I just want to say thank you. It's been a long time since anyone worried about me."

"Um—okay. Sure."

Swallowing a huge lump in her throat, she bolted for his apartment.

Before Teague even opened his eyes, he managed to take stock of his situation. There was light on the other side of his eyelids, so he'd slept through the night without stirring, except for the times that Dani had roused him to make sure he could be awakened. He wasn't on her couch; he remembered now that he'd tried several times to rouse himself enough to move, but she'd pushed him back down on the pillows and ordered him to stay where he was.

He hurt. His face hurt, his ribs hurt, his ankle hurt—and come to think about it, so did most of the parts in between. Dani had given him over-the-counter painkillers a couple of times during the night, but whatever benefit they had provided had long since worn off.

A sound from the doorway brought his eyes open, at least as far as he could force his eyelids up. Dani stood there looking at him uncertainly, as if trying to decide if he was awake. Or alive.

He forced a smile. "'Morning. What time is it?"

"Just after eight. How are you feeling?"

If he answered with complete candor, she'd start nagging him about going to the hospital again. He settled for a vague, "I'll live. You look dressed to go out. Are you leaving?"

She nodded with a frown. "I have a class this morning that I can't miss. I can ask Hannah to come sit, if she's home...."

"You will not hire a babysitter for me." He pushed himself to a sitting position, unable to completely stifle a groan when his abused ribs protested. "I'll be fine."

She hurried to his side. "You can barely move."

"I'm just stiff. I'll take another hot shower. Or maybe soak in a tub for a while." He wore black sweatpants, a gray T-shirt and white socks, in addition to the stretch bandages around his ribs and ankle, all things she had brought from his apartment the night before. The clothes hid the worst of his bruises, but he couldn't suppress a grimace when he swung his legs off the side of the bed.

Dani put a hand on his shoulder. "You should probably just rest. I'll bring you something to eat and some more painkillers before I go. I don't have to leave for another half hour."

"You've been to enough trouble on my behalf. I'll just go to my place when you leave."

"Do you have any food in your apartment? I know you haven't been home enough lately to stock groceries."

"I'm sure I can find something in the pantry."

"I have fresh foods here. Let me make you something. I'll be able to concentrate better on my class work if I know you've had a good breakfast."

He shook his head. "You're shameless."

"Completely. So...?"

"All right. Thanks."

"No, don't get up. I'll bring the food to you."

Smiling wryly, he nodded toward the bathroom. "Gotta get up."

"Oh. Okay. Do you need help?"

"This I can handle on my own."

Looking a bit embarrassed, she moved toward the doorway. "I'll bring you something to eat."

"Don't bother. I'll come to the kitchen."

Standing in the doorway, she watched skeptically as he limped away from the bed. "Are you sure you should be walking that much on your ankle?"

"Trust me. I know my limits."

Not bothering to argue with him any further, she turned and headed for the kitchen. He joined her there fifteen minutes later, feeling a bit fresher now that he'd washed up. "Don't be late to class on my account," he said, glancing at the breakfast she'd laid out on the table for him. "Really, I'll be fine."

"All right. I do have to leave now. I'll have my cell if you need anything—the number's on that pad beside the phone. Help yourself to anything in the kitchen. Over-the-counter pain relievers are in the cabinet in the bathroom, if you need to take anything. You probably will."

"I'll be fine," he repeated. "Go. Make an A."

Still looking reluctant, she gathered her things and left him sitting at the table with his food. He feigned a hearty appetite, setting his fork down only when he heard the door close behind her in the other room. To be honest, he hurt too badly to care about eating, though he hated that she had gone to so much trouble for nothing.

He looked at the scrambled eggs, bacon, toast and sliced fruit spread in front of him and thought of how different Dani was from the first impression he'd gotten of her. He had initially pegged her as vain, cool, self-centered. He wouldn't have imagined her being kind and patient with senior citizens, willing to laugh at her own foibles or unselfishly nurturing to an injured neighbor. He knew better now.

Oh, she was still high maintenance. But he was beginning to think she might be worth the effort. And that was a daunting thought for so many reasons.

He hadn't known her even six months, and he'd gone from wanting to keep his distance from her to hoping for a brief fling with her to…well, to fantasizing about even more. The problem was, he didn't know how much more would satisfy him now.

Dani half expected Teague to be gone when she returned home a couple of hours after she left. It was what she would have done in his place—waited until he left and then headed home to hole up and heal in solitude.

She was rather surprised to find him crashed on her couch, sound asleep. It looked as though he'd been headed out. His shoes sat on the floor beside him as if he'd intended to slip them on but had lain down for a quick rest beforehand.

He hadn't even heard her come in.

Tiptoeing past the couch, she set her things down on the kitchen table. Teague had cleared away the breakfast dishes he'd used. She wondered if he'd been able to eat anything. He'd looked pretty green when she'd left him.

She glanced at her watch, thinking that it wasn't all that far from lunchtime now. She would study for an hour or so and then make him some soup or something, she decided, pulling out a chair. She had no classes the next day, and school was out the rest of the week for the Thanksgiving holiday, but it wouldn't hurt to get a little ahead for next week.

She'd been studying for maybe half an hour when a sound

from the doorway made her look up. Teague stood there, clutching the doorjamb for balance, his hair disheveled and his right cheek pillow-reddened. His left eye was ringed in purple, and the lump of his forehead had several colors of bruises encircling it. He needed a shave and his clothes were wrinkled. And yet, he still made her mouth water.

Swallowing, she pushed herself to her feet. "You're awake," she said, then almost cringed because the obvious statement sounded so stupid. "Can I get you anything?"

"When did you get back?"

He sounded a little grumpy. She supposed he had a right. "About a half hour ago. I tried not to disturb you."

"I didn't hear you come in."

So she wasn't the only one falling back on the overly obvious. "I know. Are you hungry? Because I can make some soup or sandwiches or something…"

He was shaking his head before she even finished asking the question. "Thanks, but I'm not hungry yet. A little thirsty, though. And I could use some more of those painkillers, if you have any."

"Of course." She hastily retrieved the bottle of ibuprofen from the bathroom, then returned to pour him a glass of iced tea to go with it. He'd maneuvered himself into a chair by the time she brought them to him. Giving her a strained smile of thanks, he gulped both the medicine and the water greedily.

"You're hurting," she said, sinking back into her own chair and pushing her books aside. "Will you reconsider seeing a doctor today?"

"I've got an appointment at two."

His matter-of-fact response made her lift her eyebrows in surprise. "Um—you do?"

He looked at her with wry amusement on his battered face.

"Yeah. I do. I'm not quite as careless as you seem to think, Dani. I told you I'd see someone today."

"Well, yeah, but—"

"But you didn't believe me."

She smiled apologetically. "No. I guess I didn't. You were so adamant about not going last night."

"I didn't want to go to the E.R. I'll see my own doctor today, just to make sure I've covered all the bases, injurywise."

"Well. That's good, then. How were you planning to get there?"

"There's nothing wrong with my right foot. I can drive."

"I'll take you. I don't have any other plans this afternoon. All my lessons are canceled for the holiday, so there's no reason at all why I shouldn't drive you."

He hesitated a moment, making her wonder if he'd prefer to go alone, but then he nodded. "All right. If it's not too much trouble, I'd appreciate the lift."

"No, I don't mind. I've taken Mrs. Parsons to her doctor a time or two."

He blinked, then grinned, his swollen mouth twisting a bit oddly, but effectively nevertheless. "Well then, since you have experience getting us senior citizens to our doctors, I feel a lot more confident about letting you drive me."

She laughed softly, then stood. "I'm hungry. I'm going to make some soup before it's time to leave. Are you sure you don't want anything?"

"Maybe I'll have some soup, if you're making it anyway."

"Just the canned stuff. Chicken noodle or tomato?"

"Got any of those little cracker things to float on the tomato soup?"

"No, I'm afraid not."

"Then chicken noodle, please."

Chuckling, she opened a cabinet.

* * *

By the time Dani and Teague stepped off the elevator much later that afternoon, she could tell that he'd just about reached the end of his limits, strengthwise. He was deathly pale beneath his bruises, his eyes were shadowed and his mouth was set in a hard line. He wasn't exactly swaying on his feet, but he wasn't rock steady, either. Knowing how much he disliked showing weakness, she tried not to hover too closely, but she was fully prepared to catch him if he collapsed again.

Dani carried a small paper bag holding the medicines his doctor had prescribed—a painkiller and an antibiotic. Judging from the little Teague had told her about the visit with his doctor, he had been reprimanded for not seeking medical attention last night, but he'd been assured that his injuries were no worse than he'd self-diagnosed. In addition to the medications, he'd been prescribed at least a week of rest and recuperation, keeping his left foot elevated as much as possible.

It concerned her that he would have no one to help him out during the next few days. Hannah was leaving for a holiday visit with her family in south Arkansas, Mrs. Parsons was already gone and Dani herself was supposed to leave early the next morning for Atlanta. Though there would certainly be other people around in the apartment building, Teague would be alone on their wing. He didn't seem at all concerned when she pointed that out.

"I'll be fine," he assured her. "Pizza and Chinese food will still be delivered during the holidays, and there's plenty of football on TV to keep me entertained. As soon as the bruises on my face have faded enough so they won't attract too much attention, I'll probably go back to work. So don't worry about me. Enjoy your visit with your family."

She bit her lip, hating the thought of leaving him alone despite what he'd said.

An idea occurred to her, but she kept it to herself. She needed to think about it a bit more before she approached him with it. First, she wanted to try to talk herself out of it.

Teague insisted on going to his own apartment from the elevator. He wanted to lie down awhile, he said. He promised to call her if he needed anything at all. She told him she would make dinner for them both later, making sure her tone encouraged no argument. Maybe he was just too worn-out to try, but he merely nodded and said he appreciated the offer.

She waited until she saw that he was inside his apartment before entering her own. She paced for ten minutes before picking up the telephone, despite her efforts to convince herself she was making a mistake.

After a couple hours of sleep, Teague had just climbed carefully out of the shower when he heard a couple of tentative raps on his door. "Hold on a minute," he called out, figuring it was probably Dani summoning him to dinner.

Wearing only a pair of jeans and a towel slung around his neck, he made his way to the door. He'd been right about the identity of his caller. Dani stood in the hallway. She kept her eyes focused intently on his face when she asked, "I have some food ready. Do you want to eat at my place, or should I bring you a tray?"

"I'll come over. Just let me put on a shirt."

He hadn't yet rebandaged his ribs, so his bruises were exposed in all their colorful glory. Dani glanced down slowly, a frown creasing her forehead as she reached out to barely brush her fingers over one particularly nasty specimen. He sucked in his breath in response to her touch.

She pulled her hand away quickly. "I'm sorry. I was just going to say that looks very painful. I didn't mean to hurt you."

"You didn't," he assured her a bit huskily. "Um…your hand is cold."

It wasn't exactly true. Her hand wasn't particularly cold. But her touch had definitely had an effect on him. He thought it better to hide just how much he wanted her to touch him again if he wanted to share a comfortable meal with her.

Ten minutes later, his bruises and bandages hidden beneath a loose T-shirt, he sat at Dani's table, looking appreciatively at the meal she had set in front of him. She'd made rosemary chicken and creamed potatoes with tiny cooked carrots on the side. Once again, she'd gone to a lot of trouble for him.

So, which one of them was high maintenance now? he wondered, squirming a little in his chair.

"Is there anything else you need?" Dani asked, looking at him from across the table.

"No, thanks. This looks delicious. Do you like to cook?"

She smiled wryly. "If my family heard you ask that, they would fall out of their chairs laughing. I never cooked much before I moved here. I've had to learn a few basic recipes— like this one—just because I got tired of cheap takeout food."

"So what did you eat before you moved here?"

She shrugged. "I ate at my mom's a lot. And when I wasn't there, I usually went out to dinner."

Somehow he sensed that those dinners out had usually been paid for by others. A woman who looked like Dani would rarely have to pay for her own meal—unless she chose to, as she apparently had since she'd moved here. Again he found himself wondering what had happened to change her life. Maybe someday she would trust him enough to tell him.

He got the distinct impression during the next few minutes

that Dani had something on her mind. She seemed distracted as they ate, her smiles not reaching her eyes. "Is everything okay?" he asked finally.

She nodded. "I was just thinking about tomorrow. I'm leaving for Atlanta in the morning, you know. For the holiday."

"Are you flying?"

"No, I'm driving. I couldn't really swing the airfare this time. The airlines always charge so much this time of the year."

"Long drive."

"A little over eight hours," she agreed. "I plan to get an early start."

"I hope you'll drive carefully."

"Yes, I will. Um—" She cleared her throat, looking suddenly nervous.

"What?"

"Would you like to go with me?"

Chapter Six

Teague wasn't entirely sure he'd understood her correctly. "You're asking me to go with you? To Atlanta?"

She nodded. "I don't like the thought of leaving you here alone, especially in the condition you're in. I'm driving to Atlanta tomorrow morning, and I plan to come back Saturday or Sunday. My family would love to have you join us for Thanksgiving dinner."

"You're asking me to join your family for Thanksgiving."

"Why do you keep repeating that?" she asked somewhat impatiently.

"I guess I'm just having a little trouble believing you would take me all the way to Atlanta to horn in on your holiday plans with your family just because you'd worry about me if you left me here."

She shrugged, looking a bit self-conscious. "I would do the same for Mrs. Parsons or Hannah if they were injured and alone for the holiday. My family loves having company. They're nice people, even though my mother and grandmother tend to be overly curious—and have a little trouble respecting privacy boundaries at times. But if they get too nosy, all you have to do is change the subject and they usually get the message. I think you'd like my brother-in-law, Mark, and he'd enjoy having another guy besides my kid brother there to talk to. So, will you think about it?"

Teague had a firm rule about spending holidays with other people's families. He tended to avoid doing so at almost any cost. He was perfectly content spending Thanksgivings and Christmases and Fourth of Julys and Arbor Days the way he spent every other day of the year. Content with his own company for the most part, working and hanging out with friends when he felt like it. Eating takeout or the simple meals he prepared for himself, maybe going to one of his favorite diners or fast-food joints. When he was in the mood for family, he went to Florida to see his stepmother, the only family he had left. That was fine with him.

Going to other people's family events was weird and awkward. When he went with his guy friends, he got grilled as to why he hadn't married and started a family of his own by now. When he accompanied a woman friend, everyone started making unfounded assumptions about their relationship. It was just easier all around to routinely, politely decline all such invitations.

So why was he tempted to bend his own rules this time? Why did Dani's concern for him touch him so much that he was reluctant to turn her down? "I don't know…"

Looking down at her plate, she shrugged a little and said brusquely, "I'd understand if you'd rather not. I'm not big on spending time with strangers myself. I just wanted to make the offer, if you'd be interested. And when I told my mother that I have a friend who's been hurt and has no place else to go for the holiday, she insisted I invite you to join us."

"That's very kind of you both."

She shrugged again. "It's not entirely unselfish on my part," she confessed. "I'd enjoy the company for the drive. And you'd be a shield, of sorts, between me and my family. I mean, I love them dearly, but they drive me crazy sometimes. Giving them someone else to focus on would keep them from obsessing about my business for a change."

He grinned, cheered somehow by her admission. As much as he disliked being seen as injured and alone, which sounded kind of pitiful, he didn't particularly mind being used as a human shield between her and her family. For some reason, that made him feel a little more manly. Still not entirely inclined to accept, however.

He actually started to decline. But then it occurred to him that if he accepted, he would be spending eight—no, sixteen hours alone in a car with Dani. That could be both risky and intriguing. Because he had never been afraid of taking risks and had always been drawn to the intriguing, he was tempted to accept, despite the family-dinner thing.

"Let me think about it," he requested.

"Of course. I did sort of spring it on you, didn't I?"

"Yeah. Kind of. Are you sure you want me to go with you?"

"Yes," she said immediately, then added a bit more hesitantly, "I think so."

She couldn't be less positive—and she made no particular effort to hide it. And oddly enough, that pleased him again. He wanted her to be honest with him. She wasn't at all certain about inviting him to her home for Thanksgiving, but she had done so for a variety of reasons she probably didn't want to examine too closely herself.

He liked not being the only one conflicted about their developing relationship. He liked having her care about whether he would be alone for Thanksgiving. He liked *her*— very much. And that realization made him almost as reluctant to accept her invitation as he was tempted.

Deciding to take time to talk himself out of it, he finished his dinner in near silence. Dani didn't have much to say, either. Whether she was regretting her invitation, he couldn't say, but he would bet she was having second thoughts. And third, and probably fourth.

"Oh, I made dessert," she said, after she had cleared away their emptied dinner plates. She turned away and in a few moments returned with a small plate that she slid in front of him. "Chocolate pie. I hope you like it."

He took one look at the meringue-topped treat and said, "Okay, I'll go."

She paused on her way to refill his tea glass. "Um, what?"

"I said I'll go." He picked up his fork. "I hope your family doesn't really mind an extra guest at the Thanksgiving table."

Turning to face him fully, she asked, "What made you decide?"

He scooped a bite of creamy chocolate and meringue into his mouth and almost sighed in pleasure. "I really like chocolate pie."

"You're going to Atlanta because I made you chocolate pie?"

He shrugged, already slicing into the dessert again. "It's as good a reason as any."

"You think?"

"Mmm." He swallowed. "I think. Good pie."

She set his refilled glass on the table. "I'm leaving at 6:00 a.m."

"I'll be ready."

"My, um—my mother's probably going to assume we're a couple. No matter how much we insist we're just friends. And she probably won't trust you right away. Don't let it bother you, okay? I've got sort of a…well, a history of getting involved with the wrong type of man, so she has good reason to be suspicious. And no, I don't want to talk about my past. I just want you to be warned."

"Your mom will hate me. Okay, I'll brace myself for that."

"She won't hate you. She'll just be a little wary of you."

"That won't last long. Not once she gets a taste of my irresistible charm."

This time her laugh was more natural. "Well, there is that."

He grinned up at her after swallowing the last bite of pie. "It never fails."

Seeming to take that as a challenge, she raised her eyebrows. "I'm not so sure about that."

"Then we'll just have to wait and see, won't we?" he murmured, lifting his tea glass to his lips with a slight smile.

Dani made sure Teague was as comfortable as possible in her vehicle for the long drive the next morning, pushing the passenger seat back as far as it would go, propping his injured foot on a soft pillow, providing a U-shaped pillow to cradle his head. A plastic cup of cold water with a built-in straw sat in one of the two drink holders at his elbow, within easy reach, and she'd even brought oatmeal-raisin cookies for a quick snack if he got hungry along the way. She'd brought that morning's newspaper, a couple of Sudoku books and a few audio discs of recent bestselling mystery novels for his entertainment.

"Is there anything else you need before we get under way?" she fretted when he was settled and belted in to the passenger seat.

"How about a big-screen TV and a football game broadcast?" he asked ironically. "Surround-sound speakers? Scantily clad cheerleaders to serve me beer and nachos?"

"Very funny," she muttered, fastening her own seat belt with a loud click.

"I'm fine," he assured her. "You've thought of everything I could possibly need. I'm hardly an invalid, you know."

She shrugged self-consciously. "Still, you can't be comfortable strapped into that seat with all your injuries. I just wanted to make the trip as tolerable as possible."

"I'll be fine. I've made much less comfortable trips in much worse condition."

She couldn't help wondering about his background. Just how many dangerous or uncomfortable situations had his job placed him in? Maybe it was better if she didn't know.

She had worried about the long hours trapped alone in a car with him. Had been concerned that it might be awkward. Stilted. Boring, maybe. It turned out it was none of those things. When they talked, it was easy, casual, entertaining. When they didn't, it was comfortable. Pleasant.

They listened to music, they argued cheerfully about the best musical groups of the past decade, they discovered some tastes they had in common, others that couldn't be more diverse.

They tried a book-on-disc, but neither could concentrate on it enough to enjoy it, so they turned it off and put the music back on. They munched on cookies and reminisced about some of their favorite treats from childhood. And then they just rode in silence, enjoying the passing scenery.

Dani stopped every couple of hours to stretch her legs, since she was doing all the driving. Teague apologized for not being able to help with that, but the pain pills he was taking were not recommended for driving. He should be able to drive part of the way back, he added, saying that he had no intention of taking the pills for more than a day or two.

Dani assured him that she didn't mind driving. She actually enjoyed it, she added.

"I wouldn't have pegged you for a compact SUV type," Teague commented, shifting his long legs into a more comfortable position in the space provided. "I'd have thought you'd drive something sportier."

She thought wistfully of the atomic-red wannabe sports car she had driven in Atlanta. She had sold it to help finance her move, and had bought this little, used SUV from her sister, who had upgraded to a larger model for hauling all the things she needed for her decorating business. "Yes, well, I got a good deal on this one," she said vaguely. "I like your car, by the way."

He chuckled. "Totally impractical, of course. But I saw it and fell in love. I downgraded a lot of things earlier this year, selling a bunch of stuff I just didn't need anymore, moving into a less expensive apartment, putting more money into retirement funds—but I just couldn't give up my car."

"Was there a particular reason for that transformation?" she asked, thinking of the drastic changes she'd made in her own life last year.

Shrugging, he said, "I realized I was spending everything I was making and not doing a very good job of planning for the future. I guess when I turned thirty-five earlier this year, I realized I wasn't going to be young forever. FBI agents don't exactly get rich, you know," he added with a wry laugh. "I like my job, but I didn't go into it for the money. I was paying for a fancy condo I hardly ever slept in, owned more stuff than any single guy needed and generally acted like there was no tomorrow. So...I made some changes."

"Sounds sort of like what I did when I moved to Little

Rock," she murmured. "I had to make some changes, too. Moving away from my family, going back to school, starting my own part-time business—those were all things I needed to do to feel like an independent adult."

She saw from her peripheral vision that he had turned his head on the high back of his seat to study her profile. "I wouldn't have thought being independent was a problem for you. You seem to take care of yourself pretty well."

She heard the slightly bitter edge to her laugh. He would very likely learn a bit too much about her during the next few days. She saw no need to share too much just now. "So, turning thirty-five was a life-changing event for you, huh?"

He grimaced. "Yeah, you could say that. My so-called buddies threw me a surprise party. Black balloons. 'Over-the-hill' decorations. A cake shaped like a gravestone with my name and birth date on it. 'Clever' gag gifts that included things like denture paste and adult diapers."

"Ouch."

"Exactly. I decided I needed some new friends while I was making changes."

She could tell he was only kidding about the last part. Mostly.

"Yeah. Me, too." And she was only half joking, as well.

"You know, the more time we spend together, the more it seems we have in common."

She laughed shortly. "The FBI agent and the piano teacher? Hardly."

He rode in silence for a few minutes, then asked quietly, "Are you ever going to tell me what happened to you to make you leave Atlanta?"

She glanced at him in surprise. "I told you. I moved to Little Rock to get my degree in music education."

"There's a lot more to it than that." He wasn't smiling now.

"I'm not trying to pry. Exactly. I'm just trying to understand you a little better."

She focused intently on the road ahead. "I'm not that hard to understand."

"You think?"

She shrugged. "I'm a piano teacher and a college student. Hardly an enigma."

He reached out to brush a strand of hair away from her cheek, leaving a shiver behind. "I would guess that there's a lot more to you than that."

"Yes, well, you'd be mistaken. Oh, I like this song," she said without pausing, reaching out to turn up the volume on the radio. "I'm a big Foo Fighters fan."

After only a beat, he chuckled and said, "Bet you can't say that three times fast."

She appreciated that he'd decided to take the hint that she didn't really want to talk about her past. She was basically taking him there, for pity's sake. Wasn't that revealing enough?

Dani had told Teague when they'd left Little Rock that they would be staying with her sister and brother-in-law rather than her mother during the visit. "Mark and Rachel have more room," she had explained. "They're leaving for a visit with his family in Alabama on Friday, but they told us to stay through Sunday, if we want, at their place."

"Nice of them. Your family wouldn't mind if you and I stayed at your sister's house alone?"

Dani had looked at him with raised eyebrows. "I'm twenty-eight years old, Teague. They know that if you and I were going to sleep together, we'd do it in Little Rock where we live across the hall from each other."

Teague thought of that conversation as Dani drove into the

driveway of a tidy red brick Georgian home just outside Atlanta late that afternoon. It was a nice neighborhood filled with similar houses, all of which might as well have been marked with signs proclaiming "young professionals on the rise." He remembered that Dani's brother-in-law was a physician, having become a partner in a family-practice clinic just over a year ago. Dani's sister had met him when he'd hired her to decorate his new home, and they had married not long afterward.

"Nice place," he commented as Dani turned off the engine.

"Yes, it is. Rachel's done a beautiful job of decorating it, and Mark hired a landscaper to put in all these flower beds. It's pretty now, but it's even prettier in the summer when the flowers are in bloom."

"Is this what you want, eventually?" he asked impulsively. "An impressive house in a soccer-mom community? Couple of kids to fill some of those bedrooms?"

"What makes you ask that now?"

He shrugged and reached for his door handle. "I was just wondering if you're jealous of your sister. Not having any brothers or sisters of my own, I'm always curious about the dynamics of sibling rivalry."

Did that sound as inane to her as it did to him? He didn't really care about sibling rivalry in general—he was just curious about how Dani felt about her sister. The simple fact was, he was interested in everything about Dani, and he wasn't sure he was doing a very good job of hiding that fact.

"I'm not jealous of my sister," Dani muttered when they met at the front of the car. "I'm happy for her, but I don't want her life."

He wondered if that was really true. If so, just what did Dani want for her own future?

The front door opened before they even had a chance to

make it to the porch. A woman rushed out to greet them, a huge smile on her face as she ran toward Dani. Teague had time only to note that she had brown hair and eyes, that she was attractive, though not as striking as Dani. He also saw how overjoyed she seemed to see her sister for the first time in several months.

The women hugged while he stood back, watching, studying Dani's face and trying to read the nuances of her expression. And then they turned to him. Extremely self-conscious of his battered face, he tilted his still-sore mouth into a smile. He knew he didn't exactly look like the kind of guy anyone would want their sister to bring home for the holidays. Even if he was just a friend.

"Rachel, this is my friend Teague McCauley. Teague, my sister, Rachel Brannon."

So this was how a nematode felt beneath a microscope. He didn't remember ever being examined more closely—and he hadn't even met Dani's mother and grandmother yet, he remembered uncomfortably. "It's nice to meet you, Rachel."

She shook his hand. "Dani told us you're an FBI agent and you were hurt on your job. I can see she understated the extent of your injuries."

"It looks worse than it is," he assured her, ignoring the myriad stabbing pains resulting from the long car ride. The thought of a hot drink and a horizontal surface was incredibly seductive at the moment, but he could bluff his way through a couple of hours of socializing. He wasn't going to fall on his face anytime soon. He hoped.

"I should hope so. Come inside. I'm sure you'd like to freshen up from your trip. I've just put on a fresh pot of coffee, if you'd like some."

"I would like that very much," Teague replied gratefully,

deciding right then that he and Rachel Brannon were going to be friends. He'd been fantasizing about coffee for the past hour.

Though Rachel offered, Teague insisted on carrying his own bag inside. It took everything he had to keep from groaning when he lifted the case, even though it wasn't overly heavy. And he was aware that he limped rather badly as he made his way up the steps to her front door. Both women politely pretended not to notice.

He almost groaned again when he saw the staircase that led up to the bedroom where he would be staying, but he told himself he could do this. He was beginning to think he should have stayed back in Little Rock and nursed his wounds in solitude, despite the opportunities of alone time with Dani.

Rachel took one look at his expression and sighed. "Okay, there comes a time when a guy can overdo the machismo. Give me the suitcase and I'll carry it up to your room. You go sit in the den and prop up that bad foot. I'll bring your coffee once I've carried your bag to your room."

"Oh, that's not—"

She shook a finger at him, silencing him effectively. "Never argue with an older sister," she warned him. "We're innately bossy, and we insist on having our way."

Dani laughed softly. "She's right about that, Teague. You might as well give in."

He surrendered the suitcase without further argument. "Where's the den?"

"End of the hallway. Three easy steps down. Make yourself comfortable."

As he made his way to the den, Teague was reminded that Rachel was a professional decorator. Everything in the house was immaculate, perfectly coordinated and yet warmly inviting. It was very much a home, not a magazine showplace.

The den was an oasis of comfort. Anchored by a large, dusty-blue sectional sofa piled with colorful throw pillows, the room included a state-of-the-art large-screen plasma TV mounted over a fireplace, espresso-stained tables, comfortable-looking swivel rockers, a wet bar in one back corner and an octagonal game table with leather-padded chairs in the other corner. A Turkish rug, blue and tan with a dark-red background, provided warmth to the wood floor. One wall was mostly tinted glass, looking out over the huge, multi-tiered patio behind the house.

Oh, yeah, he thought, heading straight for that welcoming sofa. A guy could be very comfortable in here.

He had just settled into the cushions, propping his sprained ankle on a padded footstool, when a dark-haired, green-eyed man in a blue shirt, blue and gray tie and gray dress slacks wandered through the door.

"No, don't get up," the newcomer said, when Teague automatically started to rise. "I heard the girls chattering upstairs and I figured I'd come in here to introduce myself. I'm Mark Brannon."

"Teague McCauley." Shaking the extended hand, Teague added, "This is one comfortable couch."

Loosening his tie, Mark chuckled. "That was my prerequisite for buying all the furniture in this house. It had to pass my 'sprawlability' test."

"You've got a nice place here. Dani told me you met Rachel when you hired her to decorate this house."

Grinning, Mark settled into one of the rockers. "Best investment I ever made. So, you're Dani's neighbor back in Little Rock."

It wasn't a question, but Teague nodded anyway. "I moved into her building a few months back. Wouldn't do me any good to buy a house, since I'm not home that much."

"FBI, right?"

Teague nodded.

"Tough job."

"No tougher than doctoring, I'd think," Teague drawled.

Mark snorted. "I haven't been beaten up by any of my senior-citizen patients lately," he said, nodding toward Teague's battered face. "I assume you've seen someone about those?"

"Saw my doctor yesterday. Mild concussion, a few cracked ribs, a twisted ankle, assorted cuts and bruises—but other than that, I'm in great shape."

Mark laughed. "Yeah, I can tell. You taking anything for pain?"

Teague named the medication he'd been prescribed, adding that he'd only had one that day, halfway through the long car ride. "I don't like taking them unless it's necessary. They make my head feel sort of fuzzy."

"Yeah, it would. I can give you something not quite as strong, but still pretty effective, if you need it."

"Thanks, but I'm okay right now."

Mark gave a somber, doctor-type nod, then changed the subject. "You like football?"

"More than life itself."

Grinning, Mark waved a hand toward the large-screen TV over the fireplace. "High definition and surround sound. You and I can settle in here tonight while Rachel and Dani catch up on their gossip."

"Sounds like a plan," Teague said heartily, very relieved that the evening's arrangements weren't any more strenuous than that. "But won't Dani want to see the rest of her family?"

"I'll see them tomorrow," Dani answered for herself, entering the room with her sister in time to hear Teague's question. "I just called Mom and told her we'd arrived safely, but that we were both tired from the trip. She understands. And Grandma's having a holiday party this evening with her bingo buddies, so there's no need for us to leave here again tonight. Rachel and Mark have invited us to join them for dinner, and I think Mark plans to spend the rest of the evening watching football, if you'd like to join him in here while Rachel and I catch up."

For all Teague cared at that moment, he would be content never to leave that comfy couch again. Especially when Rachel brought him a steaming mug of coffee and a couple of over-the-counter painkillers.

"Dani thought you might need these," she said, holding the plastic bottle in front of him. "She said you haven't had anything in quite a while."

"These will be fine, thanks." He swallowed a couple of the tablets, then washed them down with a few of sips of excellent coffee. Oh, yeah, he liked it here just fine.

It didn't take Teague long to realize that Rachel was still reserving judgment about him. Every once in a while he would catch her watching him, studying his expressions, and especially his interactions with Dani. Though she was perfectly polite to him, being an attentive and gracious hostess, something made him suspect that she had reservations about him. Specifically, about his relationship with Dani. He detected both wariness and protectiveness in her eyes when she didn't realize he was watching.

He wondered what made her so distrustful. Was it only an "older sister thing?" The Dani he'd observed during the past few months had been perfectly capable of taking care of herself where men were concerned.

He'd watched her with her "lap puppy" escorts, skillfully sending them away when she no longer desired their company, manipulating them with slight smiles and a few well-chosen words. She didn't seem to be the sort of woman who'd let herself get tangled up with the wrong sort of guy—but he wondered if there was some specific incident in her past that had made her so guarded and determined to be in control.

The more he learned about Dani, the more he found himself wanting to know. For a guy with commitment issues of his own, that realization was enough to make him a little nervous.

Chapter Seven

Dani turned off the engine of her car and then sat staring at her mother's house, her hands seemingly locked on the steering wheel. She was having a little trouble unclenching her fingers.

Beside her in the passenger seat, Teague cleared his throat. "So, were you planning to go in, or is your family's big Thanksgiving meal served by carhops?"

She tried to smile in response to the quip, but she suspected her sudden attack of nerves showed in her eyes. "We're going in. I was just working up the courage."

"Something scary in there? Should I take my weapon?"

His teasing began to have the intended effect. Her shoulders relaxed a little, and her smile felt more natural this time. "You won't need a gun, but it wouldn't hurt to be armed with a thick skin. My mother and grandmother could be interrogators in a prison camp. There's nothing they love more than a fresh face at the table to give them a new life to pry into."

He laughed. "Do they use torture to get their answers?"

"Nothing stronger than endless questions."

"Then don't worry, I can take it."

She almost asked if he'd ever been questioned with more violent means. A glance at his bruised face made her swallow the question, deciding she didn't really want to know.

Someone tapped on the window glass. Mark and Rachel, who had come in their own vehicle, passed Dani's SUV, both carrying dishes of the food they'd brought for the Thanksgiving meal. "Y'all coming?" Rachel called through the glass.

Dani drew a deep breath and opened her door. "On our way."

Teague reached out to lay a hand on her arm. "It'll be fine, Dani. Don't worry."

She felt the tingle go through her arm where he touched her, even through the red cashmere sweater her mother had given her for Christmas last year. She looked at his hand, and then slowly up at his face. His beautiful, battered face. And her mouth went dry.

Something flared in his eyes. His fingers tightened a bit, turning the tingle into a jolt. "Dani—"

"Dani! Are you coming in or what? Don't keep our guest sitting out here in the car."

Swallowing hard, Dani opened her door the rest of the way. "We're coming in now, Mom. We were just talking."

Gillian Madison stood at the bottom of the steps that led up to her porch, her hands planted on her full hips as she frowned at them. Her hair was a little too full, a little too stiff, a little too strawberry blond, her makeup was a little too heavy and her black pants a little too tight, but at almost fifty-three, there was still evidence of the pretty young girl she had been. Her mom was attractive, Dani thought in fond exasperation, just somewhat clueless when it came to making the most of her assets through clothing and makeup—and not particularly interested in learning.

Gillian's decorating tastes were just as unconventional as her personal style. She carried country kitsch to extremes, with kittens, chickens, bunnies, birdhouses, sunflowers and apples painted, appliquéd or decoupaged on nearly every item in her small, blue-shuttered, white frame house.

Two large wicker rockers sat on the front porch. A big vase held orange chrysanthemums, and a huge ceramic cat sat by the front door. In honor of the season, the welcome mat was printed with pumpkins, and real pumpkins sat on the steps and in the flower beds. A grapevine wreath on the blue front door was decorated with little gourds and berries and silk leaves and flowers. All very different from Rachel and Mark's understatedly elegant home, but very much in line with Gillian's effusively maternal personality.

Gillian watched Teague's approach with undisguised curiosity. Dani was aware that her mother was not above playful flirting with an attractive younger man, but Gillian's first instinct with Teague was suspicion rather than approbation. Gillian had never trusted her younger daughter's taste in men—and okay, Dani had to admit there'd been a few good reasons for that wariness in the past.

Dani had tried to make it clear that she and Teague were only neighbors and casual friends, and that there was no reason for her family to get all protective this time, but she'd known all along that her family would have doubts. She could only hope that the way she and Teague behaved around each other—with no real intimacy or flirtatiousness at all—would put to rest any misconceptions.

She tried not to think about that moment in the car, when

merely the touch of Teague's hand on her arm had been enough to make her heart do flip-flops.

There would be no more moments like that, she vowed as she carried the dish she'd brought toward her waiting mother. At least, not if she could help it.

She made the introductions, and her mother and Teague shook hands. "We're so glad you could join us today," Gillian said graciously. "I'm sorry you were hurt."

"I appreciate the invitation," he replied, equally formal. "It's been a few years since I had a traditional Thanksgiving dinner."

"Oh? You don't have family nearby?"

"I don't really have any family still living."

Gillian's guarded expression immediately softened. "Please come inside. I'm sure you want to get your weight off that injured foot."

Dani managed not to roll her eyes, but it was obvious that Teague had unintentionally chosen the tight tact. Now Gillian saw him as a poor, wounded orphan alone for the holidays— never mind that he was a thirty-five-year-old FBI agent. Gillian might still have doubts about whether he was suitable for her daughter, but Teague would be treated very well during his visit.

The rest of the family waited in the living room. Dani noticed that Teague didn't react at all to all the cutesy decor surrounding them, other than to tell her mother that she had a very nice home, which visibly pleased her.

Grandma Lawrence, an older, heavier, grayer version of Gillian, descended immediately on their visitor. "You're really an FBI agent?" she demanded as soon as the introductions had been made.

"Yes, ma'am," he replied with a quick, wry glance at Dani.

"Have you ever shot anyone?"

He had probably expected that from her kid brother. He had

probably not anticipated her eighty-something-year-old grand-mother asking the question with a gleam of avid curiosity in her bespectacled eyes. "Um—"

"Grandma." Dani shook a finger at her grandmother. "Please behave yourself."

Grandma Lawrence looked indignant. "I just wanted to know if his job's anything like that television show I like. You know, the one with the brothers, and one of them's a good-looking FBI agent and he's always chasing down bad guys."

"That's television, not real life."

Looking pointedly at Teague's bruises, Grandma Lawrence snorted. "Looks to me like real life can get pretty exciting in his line of work."

"More exciting than I like at times," Teague admitted with an easy smile. "But I can't really talk a lot about it, you know."

Dani almost winced, wondering if he was aware that he had just all but issued her grandmother a challenge.

Twenty-one-year-old Clay, his fashionably shaggy hair hanging in his eyes and the goatee he'd sported for a couple of years neatly trimmed for the holiday, shook Teague's hand then. He tried to be a little more subtle than his grandmother, not wanting to look uncool, but he was obviously just as fascinated by Teague's job.

"I'm taking business classes at the university," he informed their guest. "I've thought about talking to the FBI when I start looking for a job."

Though his mother immediately frowned at this news she was hearing for the first time, Teague merely nodded. "I'd be happy to tell you anything you want to know about the job, as long as I don't discuss the details of individual cases I've worked on."

"Why don't we let Teague sit down while Dani and I help

Mom with the final meal preparations," Rachel suggested, motioning toward the sofa. "Grandma, you'd better come with us," she added on an afterthought. "We might need you."

"Humph." Grandma reluctantly moved toward the doorway, muttering, "You just don't want to leave me here in case I start asking more questions."

Rachel laughed and draped an arm around her grandmother's slightly rounded shoulders. "I've always said there's nothing wrong with your mind, Granny."

"Dang straight. And don't call me Granny."

Seeing that Teague was comfortably settled with the other guys in front of the game playing on the TV, Dani made herself join the other women. Maybe Teague had been protected from an inquisition for a little while, she thought glumly, but that wouldn't protect *her* from being questioned the minute she entered the kitchen.

"That," Grandma Lawrence said the minute Dani entered the room, "is one fine specimen of a man. Bet he's really fine when he doesn't look like he stopped a few punches with his face."

Ignoring the mental echo of the "Agent Sexy" nickname she had given him when she'd first seen him, Dani responded nonchalantly, "You think so? He's not bad, I guess."

"Not bad? Either you're trying too hard to pull the wool over my eyes, or something's gone wrong with your own while you've been down there in Arkansas."

"Okay, Grandma. I've noticed that he's attractive. But Teague and I are just friends, okay? And barely that. The only reason I brought him here with me is because he was hurt and he had nowhere else to go for the holiday. I just thought it was the charitable thing to do."

"Some charity," Grandma muttered.

"So, what did you bring for our meal?" Gillian asked,

peeping into the covered dish Dani had carried in. Though Gillian had told Dani it wasn't necessary to bring anything, since she had to travel so far, Dani had insisted on preparing a dish, saying she would use Rachel's fancy kitchen. Gillian had given in, probably expecting a serving dish of some frozen or canned vegetable.

"It's a pretty fancy eggplant gratin dish," Rachel reported, having watched in fascination as Dani had chopped, broiled, sautéed and baked the ingredients for the rather complicated dish. "I've got to say, it looks delicious."

Dani had brought the ingredients to Georgia with her—eggplants, red and green peppers, capers, pine nuts and seasonings—parsley, oregano, salt and freshly ground white pepper. She had topped the layered dish with bread crumbs she'd crushed herself and carried in a zip-top bag, then decorated it with laced anchovies, pimentos and black olives. Truth be told, it was one of the most complicated dishes she had ever made, and she'd practiced it a couple of times at home before attempting it here—but she'd wanted to do something that might impress her family with her newly acquired cooking skills.

"I think it's still warm enough to serve, since I brought it in this insulated carrier," she said nonchalantly. "I thought it would be nice to try something different than the usual frozen corn or green peas."

"Looks kind of different," Grandma Lawrence commented, studying the dish sitting among the same Thanksgiving fare that had graced their table every year for much longer than Dani had been alive. Turkey and dressing with giblet gravy and homemade yeast rolls—Gillian's contribution—sweet potatoes with coconut and pecan topping, and fresh fruit salad—Grandma's input—cranberry sauce—straight out of the can—Rachel's broccoli-rice-and-cheese casserole. Mom,

Grandma and Rachel always provided plenty of desserts—
two or three kinds of pies and at least one cake. Dani usually
brought frozen corn or green peas, heated in the microwave
or boiled on the stove, since everyone knew Dani didn't cook.

"I don't know if your brother's going to like it."

"Then he can fill up on something else," Rachel said a bit
sharply, jumping to her sister's defense. "Dani worked hard
on this. And we're going to enjoy it."

"Okay, don't get all testy," Grandma muttered, peeling
plastic wrap off the fruit salad bowl. "Let's start carrying
these things into the dining room. Your mama's already got
the table set."

Gillian had put both leaves in her dining room table,
making it big enough to hold all the food except the desserts,
and to seat all seven diners. She sat at one end of the table,
Grandma Lawrence at the other, with Rachel, Mark and Clay
on one side and Dani and Teague on the other. They held
hands before the meal while Gillian blessed the food, and then
everyone dug in, piling their plates high with the special-
occasion food.

"What is this?" Clay asked suspiciously when Dani's eggplant dish was passed to him. "We haven't had this before,
have we?"

"Just eat it," his mother ordered him. "Dani made it."

"Dani?" Clay looked suspiciously at his sister. "You made
this yourself? Or bought it premade?"

"I made it."

"She did," Rachel confirmed. "She got up early this morning and started working on it."

"Try it, Clay," Gillian repeated.

Despite his skepticism, he spooned an adequate portion
onto his plate, then passed the dish to Mark.

"So, Teague." Grandma had obviously been waiting until the formalities of the meal began before renewing her interrogation of him. "Have you ever been married?"

"Grandma," Dani murmured with a warning frown.

"No, ma'am," Teague replied without any evidence that the question had bothered him. "My career isn't really conducive to long-term relationships. There are long hours involved, and quite a bit of travel. Some people can pull it off, but I guess I tend to get too wrapped up in the job. I work pretty much all the time, and I have a tendency to forget everything else when I'm involved in an assignment. You know, birthdays, anniversaries, dinner plans, that sort of thing. I'm gone from home a lot, and not many women are happy with that arrangement."

"A woman with a fulfilling life of her own wouldn't care about those things," Grandma proclaimed, slicing into her turkey. "Women these days don't sit around waiting for a man to entertain them or take care of them."

"Mmm. That's not been my experience," Teague murmured, then shoveled a big forkful of sweet potatoes into his mouth.

"You just haven't met the right women. Take Rachel and Mark, for example. He works pretty long hours, too, with that medical practice of his, but Rachel keeps herself busy with her decorating business and her hobbies and her family. She doesn't whine about Mark being gone so much."

Chewing on a bite of bread, Teague nodded, an obvious ploy to keep from answering a comment that seemed to need no response.

Clay squinted at Teague from across the table. "So you just move from one woman to another because you don't have time to get seriously involved with anyone? Kind of cold, isn't it?"

Dani sighed gustily, seeing where this subject was leading. She opened her mouth to tell everyone to stop asking Teague about his personal life, but he replied before she could speak.

"If you're worried about your sister, Clay, you needn't be. Dani and I are just friends. Neighbors. There's nothing more between us than that. I date, on the rare occasion I have some free time, but I'm not exactly the serial heartbreaker you seem to be implying that I am. I'm very honest about my career demands. And more important, Dani is fully capable of taking care of herself. I can't think of anyone less likely to be taken in by a slick operator."

Teague had to notice the heavily loaded silence that followed his confident assertion. Dani wished desperately that she could think of something quick and clever to say to move the conversation along, but her mind had gone stubbornly blank. Fortunately, Mark came to the rescue, for which she would be forever grateful.

"Clay, how are your classes going? Still struggling with economics?"

Clay scowled. "I'm not struggling. It's just harder than my other classes."

Instantly on the defensive on behalf of her youngest, Gillian said, "Clay's doing very well in all his classes. I'm so proud of the way he's buckled down and worked so hard during the past year. He's kept his part-time job at the campus bookstore. He's even talked about maybe going to law school, like his friend Karyn."

Teague looked a bit relieved that the conversation had turned away from himself. "If you're really interested in a future with the FBI, law school would be great preparation, Clay. They're always looking for people trained in the law."

"Did you go to law school?"

"No, my undergraduate degree was in business administration. I sort of ended up in the FBI by accident."

Because Dani was afraid that would lead to more personal questions aimed at him, she jumped quickly into the conversation with an amusing anecdote about one of her young piano students. Everyone laughed, and Gillian reminisced for a moment about when her three children had all taken piano lessons. Dani was the only one who'd really taken to the instrument, Rachel preferring her art and Clay his guitar. There had been some epic battles over practice time, their mother remembered with a wry shake of her head.

"My friend Wanda has the flu," Grandma Lawrence said out of nowhere. "Did everyone get their flu shots this year?"

Dani was the only one who didn't nod dutifully.

She should have lied, she thought glumly, as both her mother and her grandmother narrowed their eyes at her. "You didn't get your flu shot?"

"No, Grandma, I haven't had time this year. I've been pretty busy."

"And you giving all those children piano lessons," her grandmother said in disapproval. "If you can't think of your own health, shouldn't you at least consider theirs?"

"Maybe I should start reminding you of things like this," Gillian fretted. "I worried about that when you moved so far away, that you would forget important things like getting your flu shots and regular dental appointments. You've always been so forgetful of those things. Have you been keeping up your insurance premiums?"

"There you go spoiling her again," Grandma muttered in disapproval. "I keep telling you the kids would learn to take care of themselves better if you'd stop trying to do everything for them. At least Clay's finally started learning that lesson—

now you're going to have to let Dani take her own responsibilities, too."

Annoyed for many reasons—primary among them being made to look like a brainless idiot in front of Teague—Dani replied curtly, "I'm taking care of myself just fine, everyone. Could we talk about something else now?"

But Grandma was nothing if not persistent. "I'm sure Mark would be happy to give you your flu shot while you're here, wouldn't you, dear?"

"Um—"

"Mark and I are leaving for Alabama first thing in the morning," Rachel reminded her grandmother.

"Then he'll just have to take care of it sometime today."

Mark chuckled. "I don't actually carry flu serum with me to Thanksgiving dinners, Grandma."

"I'll get the shot when I get back to Arkansas, okay?" Dani said in exasperation. "Now, would someone please pass the sweet potatoes? I'd like to have a little more. You outdid yourself on them this year, Grandma."

"Oh, you like them? That's nice. I tweaked the recipe just a little this year. I didn't know if anyone would notice."

In a blatant attempt to help Dani keep the conversation away from volatile personal topics, Rachel brought up a bit of celebrity gossip that had made the news earlier that week, which set Grandma off on one of her enthusiastic monologues about how scandalously those young Hollywood types behaved, and how terrible it was that the press reported on every little thing they did. Of course, her favorite pastime was reading celebrity magazines and watching the gossip shows on TV, but she completely missed the irony as she continued to defend famous people's rights to privacy even as she dissected their personal lives in minute detail.

Dani glanced at Teague, wondering what he was making of all of this. The glitter of barely concealed amusement in his eyes almost made her laugh with him. She restrained herself to a quick smile, then ducked her head to doggedly finish her meal. When he reached over beneath the table to pat her knee, she nearly choked on a bite of dressing.

She was sure he'd meant the gesture merely to express sympathy, but since she had an unfortunately visceral reaction every time he touched her, it would be better for her sake if he didn't do so again. Not that she was sure how she was going to stop him without letting him know that much of her impassiveness when it came to him was pure bluff.

"So, let me get this straight. Your grandmother accuses you of being spoiled. Your mother thinks you're scatterbrained. Your little brother is under the impression that you need protection from men with nefarious purposes in mind. Your sister is in the habit of stepping in to help you solve problems, and your brother-in-law very carefully stays out of any family squabbles. Have I got it about right?"

Sitting beside Teague on a lawn swing in Gillian's overly decorated backyard, Dani sighed heavily. "I'm afraid you've got it almost exactly right. You must be a very good agent."

"I am," he said with a quick grin. "But it didn't take special training to figure any of that out."

"I told you once that I was trying to change the way my family viewed me, remember?"

"I remember everything you've ever told me. I just didn't quite understand what you meant at the time."

Having been relegated to "entertain their guest" while the other women cleaned the kitchen and Mark, at his mother-in-law's request, helped Clay fix a leaky pipe in the upstairs bathroom, Dani had brought Teague outside on the pretense of admiring her mother's camellias. The garden gnomes and small animal sculptures and fairy water fountain and assorted bird feeders and wind chimes that surrounded them were further evidence of what Rachel called Gillian's "oh-it's-so-cute" decorating style.

It was a clear, breezy day, comfortable enough for them in their light jackets. Teague lazily pushed the swing with one foot planted on the ground, the other crossed at his knee. He'd worn a thin steel-blue sweater with gray chinos for the holiday meal. The sweater almost exactly matched his eyes, making Dani wonder if some woman had bought it for him. It didn't seem like the sort of choice a man would make for himself.

Her own outfit had been carefully selected to please her family. A deep-orange blouse with brown tweed slacks and brown boots—tasteful, modest, not expensive enough to make them worry that she was spending too much money on clothes, but not cheap enough to make them concerned that she was barely getting by without their help. She knew the orange color looked good with her dark hair and dark blue eyes, but she didn't obsess about her looks these days the way she had when she was younger.

"Yes, well, I've changed a lot in the past year or so," she murmured, staring fiercely at a smug-looking concrete squirrel.

Teague shrugged. "Everyone changes in their twenties. It's part of growing up."

"Why do I get the feeling it didn't take you as long as it did me?"

"I didn't have a family to keep treating me like a kid," he reminded her. "My dad died when I was just a freshman in college, and after that I was pretty much on my own to figure out the hard way how to get by."

While he said that as if it were a good thing, Dani's heart twisted a little at the thought of having no family at all. As exasperating as her own could be, she couldn't bear the thought of losing any of them.

"And now you look sorry for me," Teague commented, sounding wryly amused. "That wasn't my intent."

"I know. I was just thinking how much I love my family, despite the fact that they drive me crazy."

"That's obvious enough," he assured her with a smile.

Now she wondered if *that* had been his intention all along—to make her appreciate having her family. Or maybe she was just trying too hard to read between the lines when he hadn't meant any hidden meaning at all to his words.

Maybe it would be better if they just talked about something else. "Have I told you yet about Mark finding his biological family about a year and a half ago? It was about the time he and Rachel started dating."

Still gently pushing the swing, Teague shook his head. "I didn't know Mark had been adopted."

"He wasn't. He was kidnapped from his family when he was just a toddler."

That made the swing come to an abrupt halt. "Mark was kidnapped?"

Teague had switched in an instant from a polite guest to a stern FBI agent, making Dani remember belatedly that kidnapping fell under federal jurisdiction, especially when it involved crossing state lines, as Mark's kidnapper had done. She nodded, hurrying with the explanation.

"Yes. He was taken by the family nanny. She's dead now, has been for years, but she raised Mark, so he thought he was her son. She made it look to his family as though both she and Mark had died in a flood when he was almost two. It's a long, convoluted story with some sort of spooky elements that you probably wouldn't even believe—but anyway, his older brother, Ethan, found him a year and a half ago and told him what had really happened. Mark thought he was an orphan with no family after the woman who raised him died, and it turned out he really had two living parents, two brothers, some aunts, uncles and cousins that he'd never known about. That's who he and Rachel are going to visit over the weekend."

"Wow." Teague looked suitably stunned, his attention obviously drawn fully away from Dani's personal problems now. "That's an incredible story. Did it make the news?"

"They were pretty careful to keep the details quiet, because none of them wanted a media circus over it, but it's general knowledge that he was returned to the family after years of being thought dead. He took the Brannon family name, so he had to do a lot of legal paperwork to manage that, but not much more than Rachel did to legally change her name to Brannon when she married him. He kept the first name he'd grown up with, though he'd been named Kyle at birth. He said he was too used to Mark to start answering to anything else."

"I can't imagine suddenly having a lot of family show up at this point in my life. How does Mark feel about them? He didn't remember them at all?"

"No. He was little more than a baby when he was taken from them and he honestly had no idea they existed. As you can imagine, he was pretty freaked out at first, but he's grown pretty close to them since. He thinks of them as his family now, I think. He seems to have grown especially close to his mother and his oldest brother, Ethan, even though he seems to genuinely like his dad and his other brother, too."

"I gotta tell you, this is one of the stranger stories I've heard, and I've personally been involved with some doozies.

It's rare enough for a kidnapped child to be returned to the family at all, after more than a few weeks have passed, but to be returned this many years later…and that he turned out so, you know, average and normal. A doctor, even."

"He told us he had a relatively happy childhood, though a bit lonely. The woman he thought was his mother was very shy and reclusive—he understands why, now—but still involved in his life and determined to give him as normal an upbringing as possible. He said she went to PTA meetings and teacher conferences and ball games and everything, though she always sat in the back and had little to say to anyone but him. I think he loved her, really—the way a kid loves his real mother—and I think that causes him problems sometimes now, knowing what she did."

"No kidding. Something like this could really mess with a guy's mind. Make him question everything about himself."

"That's exactly the way he described it. Fortunately, he had Rachel to help him adjust to it all. She's crazy about all the Brannons—and vice versa—so they've all gotten pretty chummy."

"Well, you just get more and more interesting, don't you, Dani Madison?"

She was annoyed to feel her cheeks warm. "I don't know why Mark's unusual circumstances would make *me* interesting."

"It's just another little tidbit that surprises me about you. And I don't get surprised very often these days."

"Well, yeah, now you know just about everything there is to find out."

He took her off guard by reaching up to brush a strand of hair away from her cheek. His fingers lingered a bit longer than necessary as he murmured, "Somehow I doubt that."

Holding her breath, she looked at him, silently asking him

not to do this to her. For some reason she seemed to be particularly vulnerable to him today. Maybe it was the holiday, the warm and cozy atmosphere with family, watching Rachel and Mark so happily in love, or just spending this much time in close proximity. Or, even more disturbing, maybe coming back home was sending her back into some of her old habits— like needing some man to look at her just this way to make her feel valuable.

That thought gave her the impetus she needed to leap to her feet. "We should probably go back inside before Mom and Grandma come out looking for us. They're going to want to play Uno or Yahtzee or something. They always pull out the games after lunch on Thanksgiving, even though Clay always tries to duck out. Sometimes he gets away with it, other times, they guilt him into playing. Hope you don't hate games."

"Actually, I like games," he said, keeping his eyes on her face as he pushed himself more slowly out of the swing. "Guess I'm just the competitive type. I never could resist a challenge."

Swallowing hard, she turned and all but bolted toward the house.

Chapter Eight

They played Uno. And Yahtzee. And a couple other games Teague had never heard of but willingly joined in anyway. He found Dani's family's Thanksgiving rituals interesting, and he couldn't help but get a kick out of her grandmother and mother, even though he could see how they'd drive Dani nuts. Grandma Lawrence and Gillian squabbled cheerfully, but incessantly through the games, arguing over rules, accusing each other of cheating, expressing impatience when one or the other took too long to decide on a move.

Dani and Rachel rolled their eyes a lot, but were occasionally drawn into the animated debates. Clay excused himself after the first game with the excuse that he had to study, an explanation Teague didn't buy for a minute, but it seemed to work for his mother and grandmother. Mark and Teague just played their turns and laughed a lot, exchanging more than a few amused glances during the afternoon.

"You're skipping me again?" Dani asked her sister indignantly at one point. "That's not fair, Ray-Ray."

It was an entirely different tone than he was accustomed to hearing from her. Younger, somehow. Just a touch whiny, actually. She seemed to hear it, herself, immediately flushing and clearing her throat before saying in her more normal, well-modulated voice, "Be prepared. I will get revenge."

He'd heard friends talk about involuntarily lapsing back into childhood habits and behavior when they returned home for visits. Funny that he was seeing it a bit now with Dani. Not that all his questions about her had been answered, of course. There were still plenty of things about her he didn't know.

They ate leftovers for dinner, and the food was just as good reheated as it had been at lunch, though the portions were smaller this time, since everyone had eaten so much earlier. The party broke up about an hour afterward, since Rachel and Mark were planning an early departure the next morning and it was obvious that Grandma Lawrence was getting a bit tired.

"We're so glad you could join us today, Teague," Gillian told him as he and Dani prepared to leave. "It's been a pleasure having you."

He held her hand in his for a moment. "It was a pleasure being here. Thank you for your hospitality. And the food was delicious. Some of the best I've ever eaten."

Leaving her blushing in pleasure, he and Dani made their escape.

"Well, you certainly won Mother over. Grandma, too. They just think you're such a nice boy," Dani commented as she drove toward her sister and brother-in-law's house.

He chuckled. "Been a while since anyone called me a boy."

"You aren't nearly as old as you pretend to be."

"Guess it's just the way I feel sometimes. A few years in

my job can do that to a guy—which is why they enforce mandatory retirement from fieldwork after twenty years. And besides, I'm quite a bit older than you are."

"Seven years? Not that big a deal."

For some reason that pleased him. Because it had been a while since he had touched her, he reached over to brush her hair away from her right cheek.

She shifted a little, as though she were suppressing a flinch, then glanced away from the road long enough to ask, "Why do you keep doing that?"

"Because I like to," he replied simply. "I'll stop if it disturbs you."

"It doesn't disturb me," she replied instantly, trying to sound blasé. "I just wondered if it was going to become a habit."

"Possibly," he said thoughtfully.

She focused fiercely on the road ahead. "Whatever."

He kept his eyes on her profile. "It's not like my touch turns you on or anything."

"Nope."

"Because we're just friends. Neighbors."

She flipped the turn signal lever much more forcefully than necessary. "Right."

Smiling to himself, he looked out the side window, though he paid very little attention to the passing scenery.

Rachel and Mark left early Friday morning, urging Dani and Teague to stay as long as they liked in their house. Dani knew how to activate the security system, and she promised she would do so when she left, since she didn't expect to still be there when her sister and brother-in-law returned Sunday.

"You're sure the two of you will be okay here alone?" Rachel asked as she hesitated at the door.

"Are you kidding? This is like living in a palace compared to my little apartment. Teague probably feels the same way."

Teague was outside on the porch, saying his goodbyes to Mark, who had already taken his leave of Dani, so the two sisters were alone for a few minutes. Dani suspected the men had deliberately given them this time together.

"There's plenty of food in the kitchen. Help yourself to whatever you want, okay? I want you to make yourselves completely at home."

"We will. Thank you, Ray-Ray. It's really sweet of you to let us stay."

"I'm just sorry we couldn't spend more time together. But Mark's family wants to see him for their first Thanksgiving together—even if they had to wait until the day after."

"I understand. We'll get together again soon. It won't be long at all until I'm back for Christmas."

"Think you'll be bringing Teague again?"

"I can't imagine why," Dani said with a slight shrug. "I've told you all, the only reason I brought him for Thanksgiving is because he was hurt and I worried about leaving him alone. Even though he certainly seems to be healing quickly."

Rachel nodded. "Mark's kept an eye on him. He says Teague's injuries really weren't as bad as they appeared, just as Teague kept insisting. But I can see why you were reluctant to leave him there alone for the holiday."

"I asked myself what would Mother do—and I knew she'd bring him home with her," Dani confessed, smiling.

"She loved having a new face at the table," Rachel agreed with a laugh. "Especially an attractive—well, normally attractive—FBI agent. She and Grandma were fascinated by him, weren't they?"

Dani groaned. "Embarrassingly so. They really don't

have any boundaries when it comes to asking personal questions, do they?"

"Oh, they have a few. Just not very many," Rachel answered with a fond shake of her head.

"I have to admit, he seems quite nice," she added after a moment. "I can see why you like him."

"He's a nice guy," Dani agreed lightly. "We don't see each other that often, but we've become friends."

Rachel's smile turned wry. "Yes, you've made it very clear—repeatedly—that you're only friends. I'll resist making any quotes about protesting too much."

"Please do," Dani muttered with a scowl.

Turning suddenly serious, Rachel asked, "So, you feel okay about staying here alone with him? Because if you have any qualms at all…"

Dani sighed gustily. "Honestly. He lives, like, three feet away from me back home. Has for months. We've been alone together several times since we met, in my own apartment, for that matter. Why would I worry about being alone with him now?"

Rachel had the grace to look a little sheepish. "I guess I'm just in the habit of protecting you. And you said yourself, you really don't know him very well."

"I know he's a good man. And I know he's not looking for a relationship right now any more than I am. So don't worry, Ray-Ray. Teague and I will be fine here."

"Okay. I'd better go. Mark will be getting impatient. I'll talk to you soon, all right?"

"I'll call you," Dani promised, hugging her sister warmly. "Have a safe trip. Tell the Brannons I said hello, and tell Nic I'll give her a call next week."

"I will. Bye, Dani. I love you."

"I love you, too."

Rachel opened the door, letting in the cool air. Mark and Teague were still standing on the porch. Both turned when Rachel came out, leaving Dani standing in the doorway.

"See you later, Dani," Mark said, ushering his wife to their car. "Call if you need us, okay?"

"I won't need you," Dani replied firmly, "but I'll call, anyway, just to talk. Y'all be careful."

"I think it was just a figure of speech," Teague said, coming inside and closing the door behind him.

She rubbed her arms through her thin, long-sleeved blouse to counteract the slight chill that had lingered behind from the door standing open for that short time. "What was a figure of speech?"

"What Mark said about calling if you need them. It's just something people say."

Confused, she frowned. "I know that."

Teague was studying her face a bit too closely. "Then why did it seem to annoy you?"

"You're mistaken," she assured him, her tone a little curt. "It didn't annoy me at all. I know my family is always here for me if I need them."

"But you go out of your way to make it clear that you don't need them. Why is that?"

"Haven't we already had this conversation?" she asked impatiently. "I told you I used to be a little too dependent on my family and now I'm making an effort to be seen as more self-sufficient. Have you already forgotten?"

"No. Just wondering if there's anything more to it than you've told me."

"Nothing you need to know."

To her surprise he grinned. "Fair enough. What do you want to do today?"

Relieved that he'd dropped the subject so quickly, she gave his question a moment's thought. Whatever they did, she wanted to get out of this house. She blamed her sister because she was suddenly self-conscious about being alone here with Teague. If Rachel hadn't made such a big deal of it, Dani was sure the awkwardness never would have crossed her mind. She hoped a few hours out would remedy the situation. "You said you've never been to Atlanta before. I thought I'd show you around a little, if you want."

"Sounds good to me."

"It's going to be crowded out there," she warned with a vague gesture toward the door. "The day after Thanksgiving is a huge shopping day."

He shrugged. "So we'll avoid the malls. I'm sure there are other things to see."

"Yes, there are. We'll have to go by Mom's house later, of course, to see her and Grandma."

"Of course. That's why you're here, to see your family."

She nodded. "I'll just go up and grab a light jacket. It's cooler today than it has been."

He caught her arm when she would have brushed past him. "Dani? Is something wrong?"

She forced a bright smile. "No, not at all. Why do you ask?"

Obviously, he wasn't fooled for a minute. "Was it something Rachel said? Was it about me?"

"Aren't we full of ourselves? What makes you think Rachel and I talked about you?"

"Dani—"

"Let's just go, okay, Teague?"

His fingers lingered for a moment on her arm, but then he sighed and let go. "Okay, fine. Let's go make like tourists."

* * *

They were sitting in a crowded, trendy coffee shop in Buckhead when someone gasped and said, "Dani-Madison! Why didn't you tell me you were in town?"

Dani looked around to see a bosomy brunette in a vivid pink sweater standing nearby. "Hello, Andrea. How are you?"

"I'm great, thanks. Have you moved back or are you just here for a visit?"

"The latter. I'll be going back to Little Rock tomorrow."

"Without even giving me a chance to hear all about what's been going on with you?" Andrea pouted.

"Sorry. I have to get back."

"At least promise to come to Cantina de la Luna tonight. A bunch of us are meeting there for drinks and munchies. Bobby's band is playing. You have to come. And you can bring your friend, of course," she added with an openly curious look at Teague.

Teague smiled, and Dani realized with a slight shock that his bruises had already faded quite a bit. What was left just added to his dangerously rakish attraction. And it was quite obvious that Andrea noticed.

She cleared her throat. "Andrea Baker, this is my friend Teague McCauley."

"It's very nice to meet you," Andrea said. And then added with very typical lack of tact, "Accident or fight?"

Teague chuckled. "A little of both."

"Cool. Wanna join us tonight?"

"I'll leave that up to Dani," he said diplomatically.

Andrea turned again to her friend. "Say you'll be there or I'll whine. And you know I'll do it. After all, you taught me how."

Dani laughed ruefully. "I'll think about it."

"Don't make me come after you," Andrea threatened, pointing a perfectly manicured finger. "Nine o'clock."

"I said I'll think about it."

Two package-laden, middle-aged women pushed past, jostling Andrea on her heeled boots. "Hey, I'm standing here," she protested, sighing heavily.

"Sorry," one of them muttered. The other said nothing.

"So much for Southern manners," Andrea grumbled, then shook her head. "Black Friday. That's what they call today, you know, because of all the shopping and all the profits going into the retailers' books. I think it also describes the general mood after people have been shopping in these crowds for hours. So, anyway, I'll see you guys tonight."

"I said I'll *think* about it," Dani called after Andrea, who was already moving toward the coffee counter, being swallowed up in the mob.

Teague planted an elbow on the microscopic round table and rested his chin on his fist, studying her frowning face. "You didn't want to see your friends while you were in town?"

"I didn't plan to."

"Then don't go tonight."

She toyed with the stir stick from her light, decaf caramel latte. "I'm—"

"—thinking about it," Teague finished with her. "Just let me know what you decide. I'm pretty much up for anything."

She glanced up at him, suspicious of his bland tone, but his expression was equally unrevealing. She honestly didn't know whether she wanted to go to the club or not. While it would be sort of nice to see some of her old friends again, for the first time in months, she wasn't sure she was up to any more revisiting of the past this weekend. Especially in front of Teague.

And yet there was a part of her that felt like a coward

for even considering backing down from the challenge. She didn't like admitting vulnerability these days. She had her act together now, knew who she was and what she was doing with her life. An evening with a few old friends wouldn't change that, and it was foolish to fear that it would.

"Or if you'd rather go see your friends without me tagging along, I'm cool with that, too," Teague added. "I'd be just fine for an evening in front of Mark's big-screen TV."

"It isn't that...."

"After all, being with a group of your old friends can be quite revealing."

Her eyes narrowed.

He went on blithely, "I can see why you'd be a little hesitant about taking me there, having me hear some of the old stories they might tell about you."

He was all but calling her a coward! As if he'd heard her thoughts and was throwing them right back into her face. "I'm not afraid of anything you might learn about me from my friends," she said coolly.

Smiling at her in a manner that was just short of patting her indulgently on the head, he murmured, "Of course not."

Even knowing what he was doing, even though she was almost fully convinced that she was being played like a banjo, she held her chin high and said, "Maybe we'll go by for a little while after we leave Mom's house. I wouldn't mind seeing some of the old gang again."

"Whatever you want to do," he said, and lifted his coffee mug to his lips before she could decide whether he looked smug as he spoke.

Judging by the fact that they had to park several blocks away and walk, Cantina de la Luna was obviously a popular place on Friday nights. Dani offered to drop Teague off at the door so he wouldn't have to walk so far on his sore ankle, but he refused a bit more curtly than he'd intended. "I can walk."

Merely nodding, she found a parking place, then matched her steps to his on the way to the club. He made a deliberate effort not to limp and thought he was fairly successful at it. The ankle really didn't even hurt much anymore, so he figured it was healing well enough. It was probably good for him to walk on it a bit, he assured himself.

Music poured out the doors of the brightly lit club as patrons went in and out. Despite the name, the decor wasn't overly cutesy in the Southwestern theme. Colored lights and tile floors and a few colorful Mexican prints were the primary decorations. Red chili peppers were the one consistent decorating theme, hung from strings from the ceiling, painted on doors, printed on menus and napkins, gleaming in pepper-shaped lights behind the massive wooden bar.

Tables were crowded inside the place, and Teague imagined they were very close to the fire department's limit of approved customers. The atmosphere seemed cheery despite the necessary jostling. The music from the four-piece modern rock band on the small stage was loud, but not so deafening to make conversation impossible. The tantalizing smells of sizzling fajitas and tart margaritas hung in the air, making Teague's mouth water even though he'd just had another big meal with Dani's mother and grandmother.

He'd noticed that Dani had been a bit reluctant to tell her mother about her plans for the evening, doing so only when Gillian had suggested another round of games after dinner. Gillian had been visibly disappointed that Dani wouldn't be spending the evening there. Teague had sensed that there was even more to her disapproval. She hadn't seemed to like the idea of Dani joining her old friends this evening. And now, of course, he was curious about why that was. Were Dani's cronies really that bad, or had he misread Gillian's reaction altogether?

He and Dani had both changed from the casual jeans and sweaters they'd worn for sightseeing. He'd donned a pair of gray slacks and a black shirt, while Dani now wore a vivid red sweater with a deep scoop neckline and black pants with sky-high stiletto-heeled boots. Clubbing clothes. Had she brought them along in case an occasion like this would crop up, or had she raided her sister's closet? Either way, she looked fantastic in them. So good that he was having trouble looking anywhere else.

She led him straight to a big table on one side of the room—a cluster of tables, actually, all pulled together to allow the rowdy group of perhaps ten people occupying them to see each other. It looked as though these were regulars, and that Dani knew all of them, judging from the way she was greeted with squeals and hugs and a few enthusiastic male kisses that made Teague's eyebrows draw down.

She introduced him with a careless wave of her hand, and two chairs magically appeared for them. Teague gave a drink order to a server, and saw Dani do the same, though he couldn't hear what she requested. Several of the people around them had nachos and fajitas spread in front of them, but neither Dani nor Teague wanted anything more to eat.

"So, Tim," some guy Teague thought was named Len, but could be Glen, asked over the noise, "you dating Dani?"

"It's Teague. And no," he said for what felt like the hundredth time since he'd arrived in Georgia, "Dani and I are just friends."

"Huh. So, you work together or something back in—where is it she lives now?"

"Little Rock. And no, we don't work together. We live in the same apartment building."

"Cool. So, uh—" The guy was obviously trying to be nice to the newcomer, but not very good at coming up with small talk. "What do you do back in Little Rock?"

He'd been known to make up something, just to avoid the fallout of admitting what he really did. This time he braced himself and answered honestly—mostly because he wanted to see how Dani's friends reacted. "I'm with the FBI."

"Dude. Seriously?"

"Yeah." Teague accepted his drink from the returned server with a smile of thanks, then glanced back at Len/Glen. "What about you?"

"Oh, I work at Computer Kingdom selling mobile phone service. But, seriously, Tim, you work for the FBI? Are you, like, an office worker or something? Or are you really an agent?"

"I'm an agent." Teague realized the group around him had suddenly gone quiet, listening to his conversation with the younger man. He glanced at Dani, who was sipping her white wine and studying him over the rim of her glass as if to let him know he was on his own with this topic.

"You're an FBI agent?" Andrea, the woman he'd met earlier, asked, looking wide-eyed from Teague to Dani and back again. "Dani, why didn't you tell me? That's so exciting."

Teague was accustomed to people reacting in varying ways when they learned of his job. Some were intimidated, some fascinated, wanting to know if his life was like the version of the FBI seen on TV or in films. There were always a few, of course, who didn't like anyone in law enforcement, seeing them as symbols of authority or oppression. He didn't see anyone among Dani's friends who had real issues with his job, at least not that they allowed to show.

He fielded quite a few questions, some insightful, some just dumb, and then was relieved when Andrea grew bored and loudly changed the subject to something about herself.

"You could have told them you're an accountant or something," Dani murmured, leaning closer to him for a moment.

"Don't think I haven't used that very lie before," he said in return, his mouth close to her ear.

She laughed. "You say that to make yourself sound less interesting. I wonder how many accountants have claimed to be FBI agents to make themselves seem more interesting."

"Actually, I've known some pretty interesting accountants," he murmured. "I've got one accountant friend who could probably take on this whole crowd with one hand and drink coffee with the other. He's got black belts in several martial arts disciplines, a couple I've never even heard of."

"So much for stereotyping, right?"

"Right. The band's good. Have you heard them before?"

Something passed quickly over her face before she nodded and said, "Yes, lots of times."

Okay, what had that been? He replayed the fleeting expression in his mind a few times while she turned to answer a question from one of her friends, but he wasn't able to come up with an interpretation. Studying the deliberately scruffy-looking young men on the stage, he wondered if maybe Dani had dated one of them. There was obviously a connection she hadn't wanted to acknowledge just yet.

He found out when the band took a break. Letting recorded music keep the club from falling into the sort of silence that made management worry about spirits—and drink orders—falling, the four musicians stepped off the stage, the lead singer heading straight for where Dani's friends gathered. A tall, skinny guy in his mid- to late twenties, he wore his blond-streaked brown hair shaggy to the shoulders of the open-front black shirt he wore with tight black pants. No one would call him good-looking, with his prominent nose and acne-scarred skin, but Teague supposed there was a moody air about him that some women would find appealing.

He wondered if Dani was one of those women when the singer grabbed her, pulled her out of her chair and gave her an enthusiastic kiss. Watching as she returned the embrace, Teague felt his right hand clench on his knee. Rather surprised by how tightly he had drawn the fist, he made a deliberate effort to relax it before anyone noticed. He found it much harder than he might have anticipated to stay in his seat and try to look only casually amused that the singer's hands were all over Dani—the woman Teague claimed was only a friend.

Chapter Nine

"Man, it is good to see you," the singer gushed when he finally released Dani. "Tell me you've moved back home."

"I'm just here for the holidays," she replied. "The band is sounding really good tonight, Chris. How's everything going?"

"Great. We've got some pretty good gigs coming up. Got a new CD almost finished. Had some real promising nibbles from a couple of promoters."

"Didn't I tell you it was only a matter of time?" she said with a big smile. "Discordant is going to be big, you just wait and see."

Discordant? Was that the name of the band or one of their songs? Though Teague wasn't as interested in the answer to that question as he was in wondering when Chris was going to take his hand off Dani's butt.

"You're going to sing with us, right?" Chris insisted, bringing Teague's attention back to what was being said. "A couple of numbers, at least."

"No," Dani said firmly. "Not tonight. I'm just here to listen."

Several of her friends protested loudly, demanding that Dani entertain them with a song or two. Apparently, she had once been a regular performer here, Teague surmised, feeling another piece of the puzzle that was Dani click into place.

She looked quickly at him, her expression both apologetic and a bit chagrined. She seemed to be trying to think of a good reason to leave without giving in to her friends' request, maybe hoping he would supply a quick excuse.

He gave her a bland smile. "I would love to hear you sing," he said, adding his vote. "It's been a while since I've been to a karaoke bar."

A few indrawn breaths hissed in response to his words. The way everyone acted, he might as well have insulted her mama as to compare her to a karaoke singer. Dani herself drew herself up to her full height, her navy-blue eyes glittering, and turned to Chris. "One number," she said, her voice clipped.

Though Teague knew he was going to pay for his wickedly impulsive comment later, he couldn't help grinning.

"You are so in trouble," Glen—or was it Len?—muttered when Chris towed Dani away. "There's nothing Dani hates worse than being compared to a karaoke singer."

Teague chuckled. "Yeah, I kind of thought she might."

"So you just like to tick her off, I guess?"

Laughing, Teague remembered the way he'd gotten Dani to bring him here tonight by basically challenging her courage. "Apparently, I do. I think it's mutual, though," he added, frowning as he saw that Dani was now kissing another member of the band.

"You have heard her sing, haven't you?" Andrea asked, sliding into the seat next to Teague that Dani had just vacated.

"No, I haven't had that pleasure."

"So you really don't know her all that well."

"Like I said, we're just casual friends."

"And yet you came with her to her family's Thanksgiving?"

He shrugged. "I didn't have anyplace else to go. No family of my own."

Her expression turned exaggeratedly sympathetic. She was an attractive woman—primarily because of her skill with makeup and clothing selections—but Teague had very little reaction when she rested a hand on his thigh. "That's so sad," she murmured, leaning just a little closer to him. "I'm glad you could join us here tonight."

"Yes, so am I," he murmured, watching as Dani climbed onto the stage. Around the club several people applauded, signifying that they recognized her and were pleased at the prospect of hearing her sing again.

"I don't suppose you get to Atlanta very often on your own?"

"Um, no," he said, still watching Dani. "I've never actually been to Atlanta before."

"Oh. Well, if you ever want a personally guided tour…"

He glanced at Andrea's warm smile, thinking that he was an idiot. Here was exactly the type of woman he'd been thinking he needed lately—attractive, fun, available, probably not looking for anything permanent any more than he was. And yet, he couldn't look away from Dani, who couldn't be more opposite to what he needed in his life at this point.

Andrea seemed to realize what was going on with him. With a slight sigh, she turned to watch Dani take her place at the microphone after consulting for a few moments with the band.

Teague didn't know what he expected. An old ballad, maybe. Something recorded by Celine Deon or Faith Hill. He was a bit surprised when Dani started belting "Bring Me to

Life" instead. And wow, could she sing! Her rich, throaty voice could give Amy Lee a run for her money, as far as Teague was concerned—and he actually liked Evanescence. He had to grudgingly admit that Chris did an excellent job with the backup part of the song. Their rocking performance soon had the whole audience moving in their seats, and the applause afterward was thunderous.

She didn't get away with doing just the one song she'd agreed to. Her fans demanded an encore. Giving in graciously, she crooned Jewel's "Foolish Games," proving she was just as talented at soulful ballads as she was at the harder numbers.

Damn, but she looked good up there in the spotlight, her long brown hair gleaming around her beautiful face, her red and black outfit suitably dramatic for the stage. She held the microphone with the ease of familiarity, and swayed without a trace of self-consciousness in time to the beat.

"Wanna' rethink that karaoke comment now?"

Teague smiled wryly at the guy whose name he still wasn't sure about. "Oh, yeah. She's amazing."

Dani's friend nodded. "I don't think there's any doubt she could have had a successful singing career, if she'd wanted it. I guess she just didn't want it enough. She just suddenly quit singing here and a couple of months later she moved to Arkansas. Andrea says she doesn't think Dani sings there at all. Is that true?"

Shrugging, Teague looked back at the stage, where Dani was taking her bows to another round of applause. This time, she insisted on leaving the stage. The band immediately started another tune, obviously a popular one of their own judging by the satisfaction expressed by the audience.

Teague watched Dani make her way through the tables toward him, stopping several times to acknowledge compliments and return greetings. He realized that he had reached two conclusions while watching her perform. First, that there must have been a major event that had caused a woman with Dani's talent to stop performing and change her life as much as she had when she'd moved away from Atlanta. And second, that he wanted her.

Despite the possible complications, despite the reasons he knew he shouldn't get involved with her, despite the objections he was quite sure she would make if she knew the direction his thoughts had taken, he wanted her. And Teague McCauley had a pretty impressive history of getting what he wanted when he set his mind to it.

Dani kept glancing at Teague as she drove toward her sister's house less than an hour after her impromptu performance. He had said very little since she had returned from the stage, other than to tell her that he'd been impressed with her singing. When she'd told him shortly afterward that she was tired and ready to go, he'd merely stood, said his polite goodbyes to her friends and escorted her out of the club.

He hadn't spoken half a dozen words since they'd gotten into the car.

"So," she said, suddenly uncomfortable with the silence, "my friends weren't so bad, were they?"

"They seemed nice enough," he acknowledged. "Bit of a party crowd, aren't they?"

"Oh, they live to party. All of them have jobs, of course— well, most of the time—but they live for the weekends, when they get together to drink and play. I was invited to half a dozen parties tomorrow night at various peoples' houses and apartments."

"Yeah, so was I."

Looking ahead at the road, she asked casually, "I guess Andrea was one of the inviters? I noticed she took my chair pretty quickly when I left it."

"She didn't ask me to a particular party, no."

"Bet she made it clear enough that she wouldn't mind you asking her out, though. It was fairly obvious that she's attracted to you. Especially when she found out what you do. She's got a thing for cops and firefighters and rescue workers—you know, heroic types."

"Mmm."

She didn't know what that sound meant. She didn't get the feeling that he was particularly interested in Andrea, but what did she know when it came to Teague's tastes in women?

"I guess you know now why I was hesitant to go there tonight," she said.

"You figured you'd be pressured into singing?"

"Yeah. I used to have a part-time job singing there. I was never a part of the band that you heard tonight, but we were all friends and I sang with them occasionally. We did those two numbers in a charity show not long before I moved away, which was why we still remembered them fairly well."

"I'd say you remembered them very well."

So, maybe it hadn't been his type of music, she thought, a little miffed by his lack of accolades about her singing. She was accustomed to glowing reviews after a performance, and she knew she'd sung well tonight. Perhaps her voice wasn't to Teague's taste. Not everyone liked the same kind of music, of course.

He said very little more during the remainder of the drive. She parked in the garage, in the space usually accompanied by her brother-in-law's car, and they entered the house through the kitchen. She was trying very hard not to pout;

she'd thought she'd come so far from her former attention- and approval-craving self that his lack of enthusiasm shouldn't hurt her feelings.

"Well," she said, turning toward him at the foot of the stairs. "It's getting late. I guess I'll turn in."

He moved a couple of steps closer to her, his eyes focused intently on her face. "Hang on a minute."

Very aware of his nearness, she cleared her throat silently before asking, "Is there something else you need?"

"As a matter of fact…" He lifted a hand to brush her cheek very lightly with the tips of his fingers.

Warmth seeped through her skin in response to his touch. She almost shivered, but managed to control the reaction.

"What is it, Teague?" she asked, her voice steady enough to satisfy her.

"There's something I need you to know. You're not inter- ested, you tell me to back off, and I will. Nothing will change between us. There won't be an awkward moment. But I need you to know, I'm not looking at you as just a friend tonight. Haven't been for a while now."

Her heart did a quick backflip in her chest. "We had an agreement."

"Not exactly. But it's up to you if you want to take this any further, Dani. I've never pushed myself on any woman and I don't intend to start now. I just put my cards on the table and let you decide whether you want to call or fold."

The analogy made her blink, and then she blurted the first words that popped into her head, "I thought you said I was too high maintenance."

He smiled. "I'm not taking that back. Doesn't keep me from wanting you, though."

Her heart thumped again. "I'm not interested in a relationship right now, Teague. I'm trying to get my life in order, finish my education, start a new career. I won't jeopardize any of that."

Not again, she almost added.

He shook his head. "I didn't say I was looking for a relationship, either," he reminded her, his tone even and matter-of-fact. "You know about my job, how much it demands from me, how little time I have left over for anyone else. This thing between us has nothing to do with the future—or the past, for that matter. It's only about now. And right now I want you."

He kept saying that. And every time he did, her entire body responded.

"When—" She stopped to clear her throat. "When did you come to this conclusion?"

"The first time I saw you," he replied with a shrug. "I managed to keep it to myself until tonight. Until I saw you up on that stage. I knew then I was fighting a losing battle."

"You liked my performance?" she couldn't help asking.

His eyebrows rose. "Fishing?"

Her cheeks warmed, just a little. "No, I—"

"Because I loved your performance, Dani. You have one of the most beautiful and unique voices I've ever heard, and I could listen to you sing for hours. I wasn't the only one in the audience who felt that way. I don't know why you chose not to pursue a vocal career, but surely you knew it was a viable option. You're that good."

A little more of her resistance to him crumbled. Apparently, she *was* still a little shallow when it came to her music. But she hadn't craved his approval, she reminded herself quickly. She'd been just fine when she thought he hadn't cared for her singing.

He brushed her cheek again. "Don't look so serious. You don't have to make any decisions right now. I just wanted you to think about it. You should be used to men feeling this way about you, so there's no reason for you to get all freaked out about it."

"I'm not freaked out," she denied immediately, her pride piqued again. "I just haven't decided what I want to do about it."

He nodded. "You let me know when you make up your mind."

He turned then toward the staircase. "Get some rest, Dani. We have a long drive ahead tomorrow. I'll see you in the morning."

That was it? She watched in bewilderment as he climbed the stairs without even looking back at her, his limp hardly noticeable now. He wasn't going to try to charm or seduce her? No practiced lines or masculine pleading? Just a flat-out statement that he wanted her, if she was interested in strictly a "friends-with-benefits" situation. And that nothing needed to change between them if she decided that wasn't what she wanted.

While she supposed she appreciated his candor, she wasn't sure how she felt about what he'd said. She took her time setting the security alarm for the night and turned out the downstairs lights, mentally replaying the highlights of their conversation.

No strings. No past. No future. Just now. It was exactly what she had sought from the few men she had dated for the past year and a half. Since Kurt.

But she wouldn't think about Kurt now. Teague and Kurt were nothing alike, other than both being strong-willed, hard-headed Alpha-male types. But where Kurt had been posses-sive and controlling, Teague seemed almost the opposite. Kurt had been deceptive, Teague was almost compulsively honest. Teague would be no easier to control than Kurt had been, which gave her reason for concern, but maybe she wouldn't have to worry so much that Teague would take over her life if she wasn't careful, as Kurt had tried to do.

Teague didn't want to own her. He just wanted her. For now.

But what if that was only what he said because he'd thought that was what she wanted to hear? She bit her lip as she slowly climbed the stairs. What if he changed once he thought he had her where he wanted her? What if, like Kurt, he had a talent for keeping his real self hidden behind a charming facade?

Not that Teague had ever tried to charm her, she thought wryly, glancing at his closed bedroom door as she entered the one in which she had been sleeping. Kurt had flattered and romanced her from the beginning, playing directly to the weaknesses and vulnerabilities he had sensed in her. Teague had been blunt, sometimes distant and occasionally even terse.

Maybe he had sensed that she was more vulnerable to that approach now than to being romanced. Or maybe she was thinking about all of this entirely too much, she thought with an impatient shake of her head.

She had changed since the debacle with Kurt. She would never allow herself to get into a mess like that again with any man, Teague included. She was in charge of her life these days, and she liked it that way. If she wanted a man's companionship, she would accept it. She wouldn't go out of her way to please him, and she wouldn't go to any special effort to hold on to him. When she wanted it to end, it would end. And if he was the one who left first, that was fine, too. His loss, not hers.

Nodding in satisfaction at that agenda, she slipped on her favorite dark-green silk nightgown and brushed her hair until it fell in soft waves to her shoulders. She wondered if Teague was asleep yet. He certainly hadn't lingered after making his wishes known. He'd said it was up to her what happened next. That he would give her plenty of time to make up her mind. He probably wasn't expecting her to do so tonight.

Without conscious planning, she opened her door and stepped out into the hallway. Teague's door was still closed. She stood outside it, frowning at it, one bare foot poised to take her back to her own room, one hand ready to knock on his door if she ever made up her mind to do so.

The door opened suddenly without her doing a thing or making a sound. Dressed only in dark-blue plaid pajama bottoms, Teague stood in the doorway, searching her face. "Are you coming in, or were you planning to just stand there all night?"

Her terms, she reminded herself, stiffening her spine. "I was thinking about coming in," she said, her voice even and steady. "But this is only about now. Tonight. Once we get back to Little Rock, everything will probably go back to the way it was between us."

He shrugged, his gaze roaming now, down her body and then slowly back up to her face. She felt almost as if it had been his hands making that leisurely journey of exploration. Heat pooled deep inside her, giving her the impetus to take a step forward even as he said, "If tonight's all we've got, then let's not waste any more of it just standing here staring at each other."

But he was so nice to stare at, with his tanned skin, lightly furred chest, well-defined muscles and flat, firm abdomen. Deciding he would be even better to touch, she reached out to him. "Who's wasting time now?"

He pulled her into his arms and covered her mouth with his in a kiss that made her bare toes curl. She knew right then that this night was going to be spectacular, no matter what happened between them afterward.

* * *

Dani woke just before dawn. The very faintest gleam of daylight seeped through the curtains, letting her see Teague lying all tousled and sprawled beside her.

He lay on his back, his face turned toward her, his lashes dark against his still-faintly bruised cheeks. A stubble of morning beard darkened the lower half of his face, and his lips—those beautifully shaped, oh-so-talented lips—were slightly parted in sleep. The sheet lay low on his belly, baring him to the navel.

She reached out to lay a hand flat against his chest, feeling his heart beating steadily against her palm. Her own pulse quickened.

Teague's eyelids flew upward at her touch, his gaze clear, his voice only slightly husky when he asked, "Again?"

She smiled and draped herself over him. "Again."

His fist clenching in her tumbled hair, he kissed her deeply, then murmured against her lips, "I was right. You *are* high maintenance."

"Is that a complaint?" she asked, undulating against him.

He arched upward, his voice hoarse now. "No, ma'am."

Smiling against his mouth, she laughed, the sound quickly smothered by another thorough, probing kiss.

They had breakfast with Dani's mother and grandmother before they set out on their long drive home.

"Did y'all have fun with Dani's friends last night?" Grandma Lawrence asked as she buttered a homemade biscuit.

Teague nodded and sliced into the thick western omelet Gillian had placed in front of him. "Yes, we had a very nice time."

"They're all kind of flaky. Dani always did hang out with the party crowd."

"They're my friends, Grandma," Dani complained, though

without any real heat in her voice. She seemed to be arguing more out of habit than offense. "They're perfectly decent people."

"Didn't say they weren't," her grandmother retorted. "Just said they're flakes."

"Mother," Gillian said repressively. "Don't start anything on their last morning here. Let's just have a nice breakfast."

"I'm *trying* to have a nice breakfast," the older woman replied indignantly. "Just making conversation with Teague, that's all. Trying to find out if he's had a good time."

"I've had a great time," Teague answered without looking at Dani. "The best Thanksgiving I've had in years."

That made both Gillian and her mother beam at him as though they took full credit for his good mood, which almost made him laugh.

"I'm so glad," Gillian said. "We've enjoyed having you here with us. It's just a shame not to have any family during the holidays. What will you do for Christmas?"

"Mother." This time it was Dani who muttered the warning.

"If I'm not working, I'll probably fly to Florida to see my stepmother," Teague answered easily. "I try to see her a couple of times a year, but it's hard to plan even that far ahead when I don't know what's going to crop up next on the job."

"I can imagine." Clucking her tongue, Gillian shook her head. "Have you thought about a more stable career, dear?"

"Teague, if you've finished your breakfast, we really should get on the road," Dani said abruptly, reaching for his almost-empty plate. "We have a long drive ahead."

Looking startled, her mother protested, "There's no need to rush him out the door, Dani. Maybe he would like another cup of coffee or another biscuit."

"I told you we could only stay for a little while," Dani reminded her, rising.

Playing along, Teague spared only one regretful glance at the remaining homemade flaky biscuits before pushing himself away from the table. "We really should be on our way," he said, earning himself a quick, grateful glance from Dani. "You know how dangerous it is to drive too tired."

He had—rather masterfully, in his own opinion—chosen the one argument they couldn't counter. Neither Gillian nor Grandma Lawrence would argue that Dani and Teague should linger at the risk of their very lives.

Fifteen minutes later, after a few last goodbyes and random bits of maternal advice, Dani was again behind the wheel, Teague once again in the passenger seat. Dani turned on a modern rock radio station and cranked up the volume, precluding immediate conversation. Figuring she needed to unwind a bit, not to mention that she had been visibly on edge since they'd left her sister's house that morning, Teague sat back in his seat and waited until she was ready to talk.

She drove to a service station just at the entrance to the freeway, some ten minutes from her mother's house. "I need to fill up," she said, the first words she had spoken since starting the car.

"Let me do it," he said, reaching for his door handle. "I'll get this tank."

"No, you paid last time," she argued, shaking her head firmly, her own door already open. "I've got this one."

"Look, you and your family have put me up, fed me, entertained me. The least I can do is buy gas."

"I've got it, Teague," Dani said, an edge to her voice that warned him not to push her. "Just wait here, okay?"

Thinking that he would fill her tank next time if it meant tying her to the steering wheel while he did so, he frowned and sat back in his seat.

He was looking out the passenger window when he heard a man's voice on the other side of the car call out Dani's name. He glanced idly around, wondering if it was someone he had met. He didn't recognize the dark-haired, broad-shouldered, bodybuilder type approaching the vehicle, but something about the way Dani stiffened got his attention.

"I didn't know you were in town," the guy said, apparently not aware of how clearly his voice carried into her SUV. "Who's the guy?"

Dani's reply was softer but still audible to Teague. "That's none of your business, Kurt. And I'm really not interested in chatting with you, so why don't you get lost."

Teague had seen Dani be cool, discouraging, even rude occasionally, but he'd never heard this much unadulterated hostility in her voice. He unsnapped his seat belt.

"C'mon, Dani, you aren't afraid to talk to me, are you?" Kurt asked silkily.

"I'm not afraid. Just annoyed. I told you I never wanted to see you again, and I meant that literally."

Kurt leaned an elbow on the hood of her SUV and chuckled with a patronizing indulgence that made Teague reach for his door handle. "Now, honey, we both knew you didn't mean it then, and you don't now. We had a great thing until that little spat."

"Little spat? You son of a bitch, you gave me a black eye."

Teague opened his door.

Chapter Ten

Kurt winced ruefully in response to Dani's furious accusation. "I know, baby, and I apologized over and over. I was frustrated, you were so mad you were out of control and everything just got out of hand. I would never let anything like that happen again. And, anyway, Deb and I are officially divorced, so she's no threat to you now."

Shoving the gas nozzle back into its holder, she turned to twist the gas cap back onto her car. She was already angry that he'd had the nerve to approach her as if nothing had ever happened between them, but that "you were out of control" comment made her blood boil. It had taken her too long to convince herself that being struck by him had not been her own fault. She wouldn't let him start blaming her again now. "This conversation is over, Kurt. I'm leaving."

He smiled. "Back to Arkansas? I heard that was where you ran to after we broke up. I understood why you did it—and I got the message, loud and clear, which is why I finally left Deb. I knew you'd be back when you cooled down. I heard you sang at the club last night. I was sorry I missed it. You probably thought I would be there."

He lowered his voice enticingly. "So what do you say you and I go have a drink somewhere and talk? We'll remember all the good times, think about what we could have again…"

Dani shook her head in utter disbelief. "You are absolutely the most delusional, self-absorbed, arrogant man I've ever had the misfortune of knowing. Get away from my car, Kurt, or risk having your feet flattened by my tires when I drive away."

Kurt took a step closer to her. "Dani. Sugar—"

Teague was between her and Kurt before either of them even knew he'd gotten out of her car. "You heard her, Kurt. This conversation is over."

Mortified by the possibility that Teague had overheard any of this conversation, Dani grabbed his arm. "I'm handling it, Teague. Let's just go, okay?"

He moved his arm, very subtly, but somehow dislodged her hand. Balancing on both feet, he studied Kurt with the air of barely suppressed danger that Dani had sensed in him from the beginning but never really seen this close up.

Kurt had never been known as a particularly intuitive type. All he saw was that Teague was slightly shorter than himself, and several pounds lighter. Not as obviously muscle-bound. He straightened away from the SUV and crossed his arms over his chest, making sure his biceps bulged. "This is a private conversation."

"Great," Dani muttered. "Let's just turn this whole debacle into one big cliché. Get in the car, Teague."

Maybe he would have if Kurt hadn't moved into his path.

"You're going to want to move now," Teague advised quietly.

Kurt smiled, and Dani realized in chagrin that he was just spoiling for a fight. That was something she hadn't learned about him until it was almost too late: his practiced charm hid a streak of violence that he usually kept well under control but that occasionally got away from him.

"Looks to me," he said, "like you lost the last fight you got into."

Teague laughed softly, the sound more threatening than a growl, as far as Dani was concerned. "Yes, well, there were four of them. And I didn't lose."

"I'm getting in the car," Dani said, reaching for the door handle, her stomach turning at the mental picture of Teague in a fight with four gang members. "And then I'm driving away, with or without you, Teague."

Reaching around Teague, Kurt caught her arm. "Honey, wait. We need to talk."

Dani tried to pull away, but his fingers dug into her skin. "Let me go."

Teague moved so fast. So silently. Like a…like a snake striking, she thought, numbly falling back on clichés. Kurt was spun around, shoved against the hood of her SUV and had his arm twisted behind him before he could make a single move to defend himself. The few bystanders around gasped and froze as if wondering whether to get involved or call for the authorities.

"Teague!"

Teague leaned over to say something into Kurt's ear, so softly that Dani couldn't hear him. But Kurt obviously heard. He stopped his struggling and blustering, going very still. When Teague released him, Kurt gave Dani one seething look, then turned without another word and stalked toward his car.

"Want me to drive for a while?" Teague asked as if nothing at all had happened.

"No," she growled, jerking her door open. "I do not want you to drive. Just get in the damned car."

"Yes, ma'am."

They had driven nearly thirty miles before Dani spoke again. "I could have handled him."

"I know."

"Regardless of what has happened between us, I don't need you, or anyone else, fighting my battles for me. I take care of myself."

"I know."

"My family still treats me like I can barely walk and chew gum at the same time. I spent the whole visit trying to convince them all that I've changed. That I've got my life under control."

"Yes, I realized that."

She shot him one quick, suspicious look. He sat comfortably in his seat, looking as innocent as a schoolboy, meekly agreeing with everything she said. "Next time I tell you to back off and let me handle my own problems, I expect you to do it."

"Mmm."

That wasn't the answer she wanted to hear. "I mean it, Teague. If you and I are going to remain friends, you're going to have to respect my wishes."

"Friends. Right."

She glanced at him again. He wasn't talking now, apparently. Coming down from the adrenaline high that must have accompanied the physical confrontation with Kurt? "What did you say to Kurt to make him leave so easily?"

Teague shrugged. "I just asked nicely."

Which meant he wasn't going to tell her.

It was going to be a long drive. He wasn't talking much about his unwanted intrusion into her confrontation with Kurt. She certainly didn't want to talk about her past with the jerk. And neither of them wanted to talk yet about last night. At least, she assumed he felt the same way she did about that.

Sighing, she reached over to turn up the radio again.

They stopped for a late lunch when Dani couldn't drive anymore without a break. The chain restaurant she selected was convenient to the highway, with a menu that was generic but consistently decent. She ordered a grilled-chicken salad. Teague asked for chicken and dumplings.

"It's good," Teague said after taking a few bites.

"Mine, too."

"I was getting pretty hungry."

"You should have said something. I would have stopped sooner."

"I figured you'd get hungry eventually."

"Sorry."

"No problem." He ate another dumpling, then set down his fork to reach for his iced tea. "So, are we ever going to talk about it?"

She fumbled a strip of chicken, then stabbed into it again as she asked, "Talk about what?"

"Last night."

She hadn't been sure whether he'd referred to last night or to her history with Kurt. Nor did she know which subject was more complicated. "What's to talk about? It happened, we had a great time and now we're on our way back to our real lives. If you're worried about me having expectations—being 'high maintenance,' as you would put it—you needn't be. And if you're under any misconception that last night was the beginning of some sort of relationship, you'd be mistaken about that, too. We agreed that neither of us has time right now for anything more than work and a very rare evening of relaxation. There's no need to even try to start something that could only get awkward and messy."

"Nice little speech," Teague said in slightly mocking admiration. "You must have been mentally practicing it all day."

She scowled. "I was not."

"Well, the thing is, I agree with pretty much everything you said. I don't have time for a relationship right now. Every time I've tried, it's been pretty much a disaster. I wouldn't want to mess up the great friendship you and I have going for us."

"Neither would I," she murmured, deciding not to even try to analyze her feelings just then. There would be plenty of time for that when she was back in her apartment, alone.

"So we agree that last night was amazing, but it doesn't have to get all weird between us now. We're good, right?"

She swallowed a sip of tea and nodded. "We're good."

"Great. Now, you want to tell me what you ever saw in that guy Kurt?"

Play it light, she advised herself. They had just agreed they were friends and that was exactly a question a friend would have asked. "You never dated anyone who made you wonder later what the hell you'd been thinking?"

He laughed. "Sweetheart, I could tell you dating stories that would send chills down your spine."

Something certainly went down her spine in response to his lazy endearment, but it felt more like electricity than chills. And she'd never even liked being called "sweetheart." But she'd never been called that by Teague before, which seemed to make all the difference. Her mouth suddenly going dry, she reached for her iced tea again.

* * *

Hannah was waiting for the elevator when Teague and Dani stepped off on their floor later that day. She carried a heavy-looking backpack, so Teague assumed she was on her way to one of her study-group meetings. Mrs. Parsons had fussed that Hannah's only social life consisted of meeting with other med students to study.

"I see you're back from your holiday," she said unnecessarily, glancing at the bags they held.

"And so are you," Dani responded. "I thought you were going to take the whole weekend."

"I was. Then some of my classmates decided to schedule an extra study session for this evening, so I came back to join them."

Dani shook her head in disapproval. "I'm starting to agree with Mrs. Parsons. You should have at least given yourself the entire Thanksgiving weekend to relax."

Hannah smiled wryly. "There is no relaxing in medical school. You miss one day of studying and you're suddenly behind by about thirty lectures. I gave up on relaxing the day I decided to pursue medicine as a career. Speaking of which, Teague, you look a lot better. Those bruises are healing nicely. How's your ankle?"

"Much better, thanks. I'm hardly limping at all now."

"Good. Try not to get yourself beaten up again anytime soon, okay? At least not until I've done a rotation in the E.R."

He chuckled and stepped out of the way so Hannah could get into the elevator. "I'll try to wait. See you later, Hannah. Don't study too hard."

She gave him the look he deserved for such a trite sendoff and disappeared into the elevator.

Leaving his bag sitting by the elevator, Teague walked

Dani to her door. Because she was carrying a bigger load than he had, having brought a larger bag and a couple of small totes, he unlocked her door for her.

"Thanks," she said, dragging her large wheeled bag inside. "It's good to be home."

"Interesting. You think of this as more home to you now than Atlanta?"

She gave him a look that was similar to the one he'd gotten from Hannah. "Don't go all psych-minor on me now. I'm not about to start analyzing the meaning of *home* after an all-day drive."

He chuckled. "Okay, we'll save that discussion for another time. Over dinner, maybe."

She frowned at him and he cocked an eyebrow. "Friends hang out sometimes, Dani," he reminded her. "They have dinner when they're both free, they discuss stuff like the psychological meaning of *home*. Don't start trying to figure out my motivation for everything I say or suggest, okay?"

Making an apologetic face, she dropped her things and pushed a hand through her hair. "Sorry. Guess I'm just tired. Of course we'll have dinner together sometime. I'd enjoy that."

"So would I." He reached out to stroke her cheek lightly with his fingertips, making a massive effort to restrict himself to that light touch. "You should get some rest. You're worn-out."

"I'm fine. I don't need to rest," she said with a lift of her chin, reacting with her usual resistance to any hint that he might be telling her what to do. He thought he understood that part of her a little better now that he'd met her family. Not to mention Kurt.

He smiled. "Then *I'll* go get some rest. Maybe I'm the one who's tired."

She nodded a little sheepishly. "Can I get you anything before you go?"

"No. You've done enough for me the past week." Giving in to impulse, he cupped her face in his hands. "Thank you, Dani. For taking care of me when I was hurt, for sharing your family Thanksgiving with me. For everything."

Her skin went a couple degrees warmer beneath his palms. "You're welcome. You're sure you're okay now?"

"I'm better than okay," he murmured, still feeling a faint afterglow of the night before. Lowering his head, he brushed her lips with his. Once. And then again.

Dani hesitated for only a moment, then wrapped her arms around his neck and kissed him back, letting the embrace linger a long time. He wanted to hold on when she finally ended the kiss and eased herself out of his arms, but he knew better. He let her go without trying to entice her to stay, as much as he would have liked to try.

"Go home," she said, smiling faintly, her cheeks still a bit flushed from the kiss. "I have things to do tonight, and I can't concentrate if you're here."

He nodded regretfully and moved toward the door. "I'll probably go in to work tomorrow. You know how to reach me if you need anything."

"You're working on Sunday?"

He shrugged. "Just checking in. I only needed a few days off to get over the worst of the bruising, and now I figure I'm at least a week behind on the job."

"I'll have to echo Hannah, then. Don't get yourself beaten up again anytime soon."

Grimacing, he looked back at her as he made himself open the door. "I'll try not to. Good night, Dani."

"Good night, Teague."

Stepping out into the hall, he closed the door behind him, hearing it click shut with a symbolic finality that sort of made his chest hurt. Snatching his bag from the floor, he moved to unlock his door, ordering himself to stop being an idiot. Dani was still just across the hall. It wasn't as if they'd just said goodbye forever or anything like that.

Sure, it had been nice to be with her 24/7 for the past few days, but it was time now to get back to reality. It wasn't as if he wanted to commit himself to a serious, full-time relationship. To have to report to anyone on a regular basis about where he was going or what he was doing or when he'd be back. If he was going to do all that, he might as well be married, he thought with a scowl—and he'd watched entirely too many marriages fail in this career he had chosen.

Maybe someday, when he was ready for a desk job—but not yet. Not while he still absolutely thrived on being out in the field, occasional dangers and all. He actually liked not knowing what he'd be doing tomorrow, or where he would be next week. He wouldn't inflict that worry or inconvenience on anyone else, especially a woman who...

No. He'd been about to call Dani "high maintenance" again, but he'd concluded he was wrong about that, despite her willing acceptance of the term. If anything, she was too stubbornly independent. Had a real thing about being in control, which could get annoying to someone who was also accustomed to being in charge, he thought wryly. While he understood a bit better now why she preferred dating easily led "lap dogs," that didn't mean he was ready to put on a collar and a leash. Not even for Dani.

* * *

Dani was very busy for the next few weeks. She had final exams for her classes that semester, in addition to a Christmas piano recital she had planned for her students. It was a hectic schedule, and she would not have been surprised if she didn't see Teague at all, considering his own odd hours. But, oddly enough, they ended up spending time together quite often.

Teague got into the habit of tapping on her door if he arrived home at a reasonable time, just to say hi and ask how she was doing. She ended up asking him in for tea or coffee or hot chocolate and they chatted for a few minutes over the beverages, catching up on each other's day, commenting on something in the news. Just talking.

He never stayed long, saying he knew she was busy and he didn't want to take up too much of her time. Occasionally, he gave her a light kiss at the door when they parted, but he didn't seem to expect anything more from her.

If he was deliberately trying to leave her wanting more, he was succeeding, she thought wryly, fanning her warm face with her hand after one of those entirely too brief good-night kisses. Had it not been for a certain look she had seen in his eyes when he'd drawn back, she might have thought he had lost interest in her, at least in a sexual context. But she had seen the flare of heat that he'd quickly suppressed, and she'd grown to know him well enough to make a pretty good guess at what he was doing. He was leaving the next move up to her. How annoying of him, she thought with a rueful chuckle.

She tried to work in some Christmas shopping on the rare occasions when she had a little free time during the day. Every hour between classes or lessons was an opportunity to dash to the nearest shopping center and grab the first item she could afford that she thought might appeal to one of her relatives. Pleased to find a big sale at an exclusive men's store, she snatched a gorgeous, lightweight sweater at a deep discount for Mark, and found a trendy fleece hoodie that looked like something Clay would wear.

She was on her way to the cash register when her attention was caught by a display of soft wool mufflers in very nice muted plaids. She couldn't resist stroking one of the scarves, appreciating the luxurious feel of it against her skin. They were marked down considerably, still a bit pricey but within her budget. She didn't think Clay would wear one, and Mark probably had a closetful of nice neck scarves.

She fingered a nice black-watch plaid, thinking how good it would look on Teague. Though early winter had been quite mild in Arkansas, January and February were predicted to be colder than usual, if the forecasters were to be believed. Maybe Teague would like a warm scarf on those stakeouts or whatever he was doing all those late nights. Could FBI agents even wear scarves on duty? She hadn't a clue, but it would still go well with the soft black leather bomber jacket he often wore, so maybe he could wear it when he wasn't on the job. For a date or something, maybe.

That thought made her drop her hand from the scarf. She wasn't buying accessories for Teague to wear on dates. Besides, they weren't really on gift-swapping terms. They were just casual pals. She wouldn't want him reading anything more into a gift than she intended.

She took another step toward the register, then hesitated again. What if Teague got *her* a gift? Just a friendly, neighborly gesture in the spirit of the season? It would be awkward if she had nothing to give him in return.

Okay, so maybe she would buy the scarf, stuff it in a gift

bag and have it on hand in case he did show up with something for her. If he didn't, she would give it to Mark. Or maybe hang on to the receipt and return it for a refund, since she didn't need to waste the money, anyway. Either way, she thought, snatching the scarf from the display, she would be prepared. It was a quite practical purchase, actually.

Deciding to leave it at that, she dumped her merchandise on the checkout counter and reached for her credit card.

Teague took the stairs up to his floor, bypassing the tempting-looking elevator. He was tired, but he needed the exercise. Now, had Dani been riding the elevator—

He shook his head and pushed through the door into his hallway. Seemed like she was all he thought about these days. Every time he let his attention wander from the job, Dani crept into his mind. He hadn't allowed thoughts of her to interfere with his work; he'd been as efficient and focused as ever. But the moment he went off duty, there she was again.

He glanced at her door. It was barely 6:00 p.m., and he figured she was probably there. He usually made a point to say hello when he got home, but maybe he should just keep walking this time. Things were getting just a little too...well, *cozy* was the first word that came to his mind.

He was getting a little too accustomed to being greeted by her when he came home, to sharing a hot drink and a comfortable conversation. And he was getting a lot too frustrated every time he left her with no more than an occasional friendly kiss.

All in all, he should keep walking. Instead he felt his feet taking him straight to Dani's door. His knuckles rapped on the wood almost as if with a will of their own.

She opened the door, and he could see at a glance that she was getting ready to go out. Her hair was up in a pretty twist of some sort, she wore a bit more makeup than usual and she was dressed in a modest, long-sleeved, midcalf jersey dress that clung nicely to her near-perfect figure.

"Sorry, I didn't know you had plans for the evening," he said, taking a step backward. "I just wanted to say hello."

Did she have a date? Another one of her lap puppies? And was it really wrong of him to want to pound the guy, sight unseen? Especially since he and Dani were "only friends"?

She wrinkled her nose. "Didn't I mention I'm singing in a choir concert at the university this evening? It's a program of Christmas music. No big deal, just something I'm required to participate in for my grade."

"Yeah?" Unclenching the fist in his jacket pocket, he tilted his head. "When does it start?"

She glanced at her watch. "In just under an hour. I'm leaving in about ten minutes."

"So, is this a casual sort of thing? I mean, would it be okay if I go dressed like this?" he asked, motioning toward the pale gray shirt and charcoal slacks he wore beneath his black leather jacket, the same outfit he'd worn to work that day.

She looked startled. "You want to go to the concert?"

He shrugged. "I don't have any other plans for the evening. And I like hearing you sing."

"I'll be singing in a choir," she reminded him. "I have only one solo part."

"I'll hear your voice in the choir," he predicted. "You don't mind if I go, do you?"

"Well…no, not if you really want to." She smiled a bit uncertainly. "Actually, it will be nice to have someone who's there with me, since most of the others will have family in attendance."

"Then I'm definitely going. Give me five minutes to freshen up and I'll drive you."

"All right." Still smiling, she closed the door.

So he was going to a college choir concert, Teague thought, hurrying to his own apartment. What the hell had he been thinking? He didn't even like Christmas music all that much. Too many fa-la-las and sleigh bells jingling for his hard-rocking musical soul.

He really had to think about this thing with Dani, he decided. Seriously.

Half an hour later he sat in the audience of the auditorium, waiting for the concert to begin. He held a printed program listing the songs that would be performed—quite a few of them, he thought with a wince, and a lot of them sounded as though they were in Latin and French—and the names of all the choir members. He found Dani's name, and noted that she'd used Danielle rather than the shortened version. It looked odd, since he didn't think of her as Danielle now.

The guy in the seat next to him dropped his own program, and bumped Teague's shoulder as he bent to retrieve it. "Sorry."

"No problem."

"Another choir performance, huh?" the older man asked jovially.

A little confused by the wording, Teague nodded. "Yeah, I guess so."

"Which one's yours?"

"Which what is mine?" Teague asked blankly.

The other man chuckled and nodded his graying head toward the program in Teague's hand. "Which kid? Son or daughter?"

Oh, man. The guy thought Teague had a kid in college. Even a freshman would be eighteen or nineteen, and Teague would have had to have been a real sexual prodigy to have accomplished that.

While it was true that the auditorium lights had already been dimmed so that maybe the other man wasn't seeing him all that clearly, Teague was still a bit chagrined. Maybe he should have taken time to shave before he came. Maybe the beard made him look older. Or maybe the job was aging him faster than he'd realized.

"Neither. I don't have any kids. I'm here for a friend in the choir," he said, trying not to sound too abrupt.

The other guy squinted a bit to study Teague more closely. "Oh, guess you're younger than I realized. Sorry, I left my glasses at home, which is why I dropped my program. I was trying to find my daughter's name."

Only a little placated, Teague nodded.

"She's my youngest of three daughters," the other man confided, obviously the chatty sort. On his other side, his wife was gossiping with another woman, leaving her husband to entertain himself by talking to a stranger. "Can't tell you how many concerts and recitals and plays and school programs I've sat through during the past twenty-five years."

"Sounds like you've been a very involved father."

"I've tried to be. I tell you, son, I've done a lot of things in my life, accomplished quite a bit, but there's nothing I'm prouder of than my girls. You'll see someday."

"Mmm." Teague was immensely relieved when the house lights went down and music began to play. The piece was heavy on sleigh bells, but it sounded great, as far as Teague was concerned, since it effectively put an end to that awkward conversation.

Chapter Eleven

Dani was to leave very early on December 23 for Atlanta. She was flying this time, the ticket a gift from her family so she wouldn't have to make the long drive again. Teague had planned to visit his stepmother, but work responsibilities cropped up, so he had to postpone the trip. He offered to drive Dani to the airport, but she politely declined, telling him she would just leave her car in airport parking.

She invited him to have dinner with her the night before she left, telling him it would be their own holiday celebration. She would have invited Hannah, too, but Hannah had already left for her family home.

Dani went to a lot of trouble for the meal, choosing not to analyze why it seemed so important to do so. She had put out a few decorations for the season—a wreath on her door, a small Christmas tree, a pretty centerpiece on her table. She served a down-home holiday meal of country ham, creamed potatoes with red-eye gravy, green beans and corn. She wasn't brave enough to try making her grandmother's homemade biscuits, so she bought brown-and-serve rolls instead. For dessert, she bought a premade pumpkin pie because she knew Teague liked pumpkin.

"This was really nice," he told her when he had finished the last bite of his dessert. "You shouldn't have gone to so much trouble when you had so much else to do this week."

Pleased by the praise, she shrugged. "I wanted to. I feel bad that you're going to be working through Christmas and not visiting your stepmother, so I wanted you to have one nice holiday meal."

"That was very nice of you. But I did volunteer to work this week, you know. It wouldn't have been right to keep some guy away from his kids when I don't have anyone who'll miss me on Christmas."

She bit her lip to keep herself from responding to that. Something told her that she would be thinking of Teague at least a couple of times on Christmas, and she was very much afraid that she would be missing him.

It really was a good thing they were going to be spending a week apart, she decided, stacking dishes in the dishwasher. She needed a little distance from Teague, to remind herself of why she didn't want her life to revolve around a man again. Not that Teague ever made any demands on her. He was just always…there. And that could be all too easy to get accustomed to, especially since she knew he could drift out of her life as quickly as he had stumbled in.

"Oh, by the way," he said when they'd finished cleaning the kitchen. "I got you a little something for Christmas. It's in my jacket in the other room."

"Oh, you didn't have to do that," she said automatically,

thanking her stars that there was a wrapped gift with Teague's name on it under her little tree.

"I wanted to. It's no big deal," he said with a slightly self-conscious shrug. "I don't have that many people to buy Christmas gifts for."

She followed him into the living room and watched as he pulled a small wrapped gift out of his jacket pocket. She plucked his gift out from under her tree as he turned. "I got you something, too," she admitted.

"That wasn't necessary, either," he said, though he looked pleased that she had gone to the effort. She wondered how many people had actually thought of him with a gift this Christmas. And how much of his solitude was by his own choice.

She opened her gift to find that he had bought her a gold charm shaped like a music note. It was very delicate, very feminine, a bauble that could be worn on a chain or a bracelet, and something about it surprised her, because it didn't seem like something Teague would buy.

"I guess it's a little obvious, but it reminded me of you," he said with a slight shrug when she looked up at him. "I'm not very good at buying presents."

He'd spent too much, she thought, feeling the weight of the gold in her hand, as delicate as the charm might be. She knew jewelry, and this was no cheapie trinket. But something about the way he had watched her open it, as though he was afraid she wouldn't like it or wouldn't accept it, kept her from voicing her reservations. "I think it's lovely. I've got a chain that will be perfect for it. Thank you, Teague."

His smile made her glad she'd decided to accept graciously. He seemed relieved, as though he'd had second—maybe third—thoughts about his selection. Yes, the selection was a bit obvious for a music teacher/student, but the fact that he'd made an effort to choose something so tailored to her interests made it special.

He opened his gift then, and he seemed pleased. "Wow," he said, running the scarf through his hands. "That feels good. I had a nice muffler, but it's about worn out. Thanks, Dani."

"I'm glad you like it. I thought it would look good with your black jacket."

Teague was still studying the classic pattern of the plaid. "You know, my dad had a scarf a lot like this one. This same plaid. It was his favorite pattern."

"Black watch? Yes, it's a classic plaid."

"He had a pair of pajamas in the same plaid. Wore them until the buttons came off and he had safety pins holding the shirt together. He was red-green color blind, so he couldn't see a lot of colors, but he liked the blues in this pattern. My stepmother finally made him throw the pajamas away. She bought him several new sets, but I don't think he ever liked any of them as well as that one pair."

"You and your father were close?" she asked, trying to read his tone.

He sighed lightly. "Not as close as I would have liked. We would have been, I think, had he lived longer. A little further past my teen rebellion years. But, yeah, we got along pretty well for the most part."

"Do you miss him?" she asked, hearing the wistfulness in her own voice.

Teague looked at her steadily. "Every day."

She swallowed and nodded. "I miss my dad, too. He and I were very close. I was very much Daddy's girl. It devastated me to lose him. As much as I enjoy spending the holidays with my family, I'm always aware of his absence now. Especially Christmas. He loved Christmas."

Teague squeezed her shoulder lightly. "I'm sorry."

She shrugged a little beneath his touch. "I'm okay. It's part of life, I know, to lose people you love."

"Yeah, but it's a sucky part."

That made her smile just a little. "Exactly."

He leaned down to brush his lips across her forehead. "Thank you, Dani. I'll enjoy using the scarf."

She smiled up at him. "And I'll enjoy the charm."

His lips touched her cheek and the end of her nose. "I hope you will."

Turning her head a little, she let their lips meet. Just for a light, friendly kiss in the spirit of their pleasant evening together.

What started as a light caress spiraled out of her control before she could do anything to stop it. She wasn't sure how her arms ended up around his neck when she didn't even remember lifting them. How her fingers managed to entangle themselves so deeply into his hair. His arms were around her, his legs tangled with hers, and there was no doubt that the embrace had become as intense for him as it was for her.

They kissed until kisses were no longer enough, and then Teague groaned and tried to disentangle himself. "You have to leave early in the morning," he muttered, his jaw tight with restraint. "You need some sleep."

She hesitated only a moment before tugging him back against her. "I'll nap on the plane."

Laughing against her lips, he nudged her toward the bedroom.

"It's a shame Teague couldn't join us for Christmas," Gillian said late Christmas afternoon. The gifts had all been unwrapped and exclaimed over, massive amounts of food had been consumed and now Dani and her mother and grandmother were sitting in the kitchen, relaxing with cups of hot spiced cider.

Clay was at his girlfriend's house, and Rachel and Mark were hosting his family that day at their house, having shared Christmas Eve with Rachel's family. Dani, who was staying at her mother's house this time, was left alone to be grilled by the family matriarchs.

Having made a solemn vow to herself during the plane ride not to get into any arguments with her mother this holiday, or to overreact to maternal advice or reproach, Dani kept her expression bland as she responded, "I told you, Mom. Teague had to work. Besides, he doesn't expect to spend all holidays with a family he barely knows. He came for Thanksgiving only because he'd been injured and had no one to look out for him."

"Having to work on Christmas." Grandma Lawrence shook her head in disapproval. "Being beaten up at Thanksgiving. Being in danger all the time. That's a very hard job Teague has, Dani."

"Well, I don't think he's literally in danger all the time," Dani demurred. "From what he's told me, he spends more time on the computer and plowing through paperwork than he does in actual confrontations with bad guys. He has to travel a lot, and he works pretty long hours when he's in the middle of a difficult case, but it's not really like on TV with danger around every corner."

It *was* a risky job, of course, and she was always aware of that whenever Teague left for work. She just didn't want to analyze her feelings about it now, with her mother and grandmother, who always tended to read too much into the things she said.

"He's a very nice man," Gillian murmured, "but I'm not sure he's such a good match for you, Dani. I don't know how well you would deal with the constant worry about him. Or with having your plans and holidays messed up at the last minute because of the demands of his job. I'm afraid it would lead to conflict since you…well, you like things to go just so."

Her resolutions evaporating, Dani asked coolly, "You mean because I'm so 'high maintenance'?"

"I didn't say high maintenance," Gillian countered. "I just meant—"

"Never mind," Dani cut in with a firm shake of her head. "It doesn't matter, anyway, because I'm not planning a long-term future with Teague. He and I just hang out occasionally because we enjoy each other's company, but that's all there is to it. We each have our own lives, and neither of us is interested in making any changes right now, so just don't worry about it, okay?"

"But—"

"I don't think Dani wants to talk about Teague anymore right now," Grandma Lawrence said, studying Dani's face perceptively. "Let's talk about something else now. Dani, did we tell you that Caroline Drennan got promoted to vice principal of the elementary school where she's been teaching? You know she's always wanted to get into administration, and she's finally getting her chance."

Gratefully, Dani latched onto the new topic. "Good for her. She was a good teacher, but she'll be a great principal. She gets along so well with everyone, but I'd bet she can be tough when she has to be."

A little sulkily, Gillian made a grudging comment, and before long they were all deep into a discussion of local gossip. Dani tried to pretend for the rest of the day that Teague never even entered her thoughts. She hoped she fooled the others, because she certainly had no success in deluding herself that she wasn't becoming more and more obsessed with him.

* * *

"I'm so bored." Mike Ferguson let his shaggy head drop dramatically backward onto the headrest of the seat in the battered pickup truck in which he and Teague slouched. "This is the worst Christmas night ever."

"It'd be a lot better if you'd quit bitching and just watch for Carlisle," Teague replied without sympathy. He reached for his insulated mug of cooling coffee and took a swallow, hoping the caffeine would clear his own boredom-dulled brain. Anybody who'd ever believed stakeouts were exciting should sit in on a few, he thought grimly.

"Carlisle's not going to show. How stupid would he be to come here tonight?"

"He's not a particularly smart guy," Teague said, shrugging. "Just slippery. Visiting his mother on Christmas is something the jerk would very likely try to pull off."

"Seems kind of cold busting him in front of his mama on Christmas."

"Colder that he's deprived a couple mamas of their kids on Christmas."

"There is that. If he shows up, we'll get him. Just hope he doesn't make us have to run or duck bullets or anything. I've eaten so much sugar tonight that I'm feeling kinda sluggish."

"Put away the bag of Christmas candy, then. Carlisle's not likely to hold out his arms and invite us to carry him off to jail." Which was why they were both wearing bulletproof vests as they sat in the uncomfortable but suitably inconspicuous vehicle, watching the gang leader's mother's house.

Mike popped another chocolate Santa into his mouth in a defiant gesture. "Eating gives me something to do, since you're in one of your moods."

Teague scowled. "I'm not in a mood."

"Sure you are. It's like pulling teeth to get you to talk tonight. I mean, I don't want to be spending Christmas on a stakeout any more than you do, but at least I'm not sitting here sulking about it."

"I'm not sulking. I'm just thinking."

"Thinking about her? The princess?"

His fingers twitching on the steering wheel, Teague tried to speak lightly. "You mean my neighbor? Dani?"

"Like you didn't know who I was talking about. You've been seeing a lot of her, haven't you?"

His scowl deepening, Teague asked, "How did you know that?"

Mike chuckled. "I didn't until just now. So, how often *have* you been seeing her?"

Not nearly enough, Teague thought glumly. And yet, in some ways, entirely too much. He wondered what his partner would say if he answered that way. Ferguson would probably laugh his butt off at Teague's uncharacteristic dithering. When it came to Dani, Teague was decidedly conflicted, wanting to be with her even as he worried about getting too close.

He couldn't predict what was going to happen between them, and that bugged his always-in-control soul. They could gradually drift apart, as both of them got involved with their busy careers, but for some reason that didn't seem likely as long as they were living in such close proximity.

As far as he knew, Dani hadn't dated anyone since she'd been hanging out with him, but there was certainly nothing keeping her from seeing someone else. She could decide to get more deeply involved with one of those guys she dated occasionally, in which case Teague would be eased out of the scene. It bothered him how much he hated picturing her with anyone else. He thought it would be extremely painful to watch her go into her apartment with some other man.

So what was the alternative? Should he try to talk her into taking that next step with him, from being "friends with benefits" to a real couple? He didn't know if she would even be interested in trying, since she'd made it clear that she wasn't looking for anything serious right now. At least, not with him. And she was probably right. Every instinct told him that any relationship between them would be volatile, and that the ending wouldn't be an easy one. It was just the way they were when they were together. Explosive.

"Dude." Mike waved a hand in front of Teague's eyes. "Still with me?"

"I'm just watching for Carlisle," Teague snapped, focusing again on the doorway down the street. "Eat your candy."

"Man," Mike muttered, digging into the bag again. "She's really got you tied in knots. Never thought I'd see the day."

Teague winced and sank more deeply into his seat.

Dani had told Teague she would return very late on the twenty-seventh and she certainly wasn't expecting to see him that evening. She'd taken a late flight out of Atlanta, wanting to spend as much time as possible with her family. She wasn't sure when she'd have the chance to get back to see them, now that the holidays were over.

It was after eleven when she climbed out of her SUV and reached in for her bags. She'd taken two large suitcases, one almost empty on the way there, since she knew she'd be bringing back Christmas gifts. They were both full now, and heavy. Slinging her equally loaded carry-on tote over her shoulder, she tried to balance both her suitcases, since she didn't want to make an extra trip out to the shadowy parking lot tonight.

Someone reached around her to take one of the suitcases. "I was starting to get worried about you."

She jumped almost a foot before she realized who it was. "Teague, you scared the stuffing out of me," she scolded. "I didn't see you there. Were you waiting for me?"

There was enough artificial light for her to see that he was frowning. "You should always be aware of who's around you, especially this late at night," he scolded, ignoring her question. "I could have been just anyone lurking in the shadows."

"I know, and I'm usually more careful," she said, resenting the lecture. "I'm just tired tonight."

"That's exactly what a predator looks for. Someone who's tired or distracted or otherwise vulnerable to an attack. I could have had you stuffed in a waiting car before you even knew I was in the parking lot."

"Okay, Teague, I got it. Now drop it, okay? I've spent several days being lectured about everything from my hair to my clothes to my work schedule, and I don't need you piling on more."

"I'm just worried about your safety," he muttered, following her into the elevator. "It is sort of my area of expertise, you know."

"Great. If I'm ever in the market for a bodyguard, I'll give you a call. In the meantime, I'll watch out for myself."

He sighed gustily. "I don't want to fight with you tonight."

"I don't want to fight, either," she conceded. Only then did she notice that he was wearing the scarf she'd bought him around the collar of his black jacket. She wore the music-note charm on a gold chain beneath her warm green sweater.

He held the elevator door so that she could exit first, dragging her suitcase behind her as he followed with the second. "Did you have a nice visit with your family in spite of the lectures?"

"Yes, I did. The lectures are just part of my family's

dynamics. I don't particularly like them, but I'm used to them. How about you? How did your holiday go?"

"Caught a stupid fugitive," Teague replied with a shrug, setting her bag on her living room floor. "He told us he didn't think the FBI would be cold enough to arrest someone on Christmas day. My partner struck a pose and told him that 'justice takes no holidays.' Our perp couldn't think of anything to say, so he just sulked after that. It was his mother that gave us the most trouble with the arrest. Took two guys to restrain her while several others of us hauled off her lowlife son."

She laughed. "Seriously? And your partner really said that?"

"Yeah. You'd have to meet Ferguson to understand. And it's not the first time I've encountered a mother who turned violent when protecting her kid, even if the kid happened to be a murderous drug dealer."

She turned serious. "Doesn't sound like much of a holiday for you."

"Are you kidding? I had a great time."

She searched his face, and decided he was only half teasing. Teague really did love his job. Any woman who got seriously involved with him would have to have the patience of a saint to have her own plans and holidays forever tenuous because, as his partner had said, "justice takes no holidays." Remembering that her mother had said something along those same lines, and had then implied that Dani wasn't the type to handle such demands graciously, Dani turned abruptly away from him.

"Wow, I'm tired," she said. "It's been a long day."

"I'll let you get some rest, then." He turned toward the door. "Good night, Dani. See you around, okay?"

So very careful not to put any demands on her time. To keep things casual and tenuous. For her sake or his own? Too weary to analyze it tonight, she crossed her arms over her chest, hugging her forearms as if to ward off a chill, even though she hadn't even taken off her coat yet. "See you around, Teague."

He hesitated a moment, as if he wanted to do or say something more, but then he merely nodded and moved toward the door.

"Teague?"

He was already halfway out in the hall when she impulsively said his name. "Yeah?" he asked, glancing back.

"Were you really waiting for me to get home?"

After a pause, he shrugged. "Just keeping an eye out. It being so late and all."

"It wasn't necessary."

"I know. I'll try not to make a habit of it. Good night." Stepping out into the hall, he closed the door behind him.

Growling deep in her throat, Dani stripped off her coat and threw it on the floor. This…whatever it was…between her and Teague was getting entirely too complicated, as she'd suspected it would from the start.

She never should have made him that first cup of hot chocolate, puppy-dog eyes or not.

Chapter Twelve

Dani wanted to stay busy enough during the next few days that she didn't have time to even think about Teague, but that wasn't easy since classes hadn't started back at the university yet and piano lessons weren't scheduled until after the first of the year. So she put away her seasonal decorations, cleaned her apartment from ceiling to floor and found places for her Christmas gifts. She packed up some clothing she'd grown tired of, to donate to charity, and shopped for groceries to restock her empty pantry.

Sadly enough, keeping her hands occupied did nothing to prevent Teague from creeping into her thoughts with disturbing regularity. She hated that she listened for him in the hallway, watched for his car when she went out to the parking lot, waited for his familiar tap on her door. She didn't want to do this. Didn't want to become too attached to him.

She shuddered as she remembered the way she'd been

during her wretched relationship, if it could be called that, with Kurt. He'd been married at the time, something that made her ashamed to remember now, despite his repeated assurances to her that he and his wife were separating and that his wife was moving on with her own life. She knew now that it had all been lies, that she had been nothing more than a semisecret mistress, but at the time she'd believed every lying word he'd told her because she had fancied herself in love with him.

In no way did she think Teague and Kurt were alike, other than both being strong men with take-charge personalities. It was herself she worried about. With Kurt, she had become unexpectedly needy, compliant, self-sacrificing. She'd sat for hours by her phone waiting for him to call her, alienated friends and family, cried and stewed when he wasn't with her. She'd almost completely given up her own dreams and ambitions during that time. Anything to please him. Until she had finally grown a backbone and broken up with him completely after the one and only time he had tried controlling her with violence.

She had spent a lot of time analyzing why she'd been that compliant with Kurt. Trying to understand her behavior so she would never repeat it. She had finally decided she would never understand completely why she'd let herself get into that mess, but it probably had a lot to do with losing her father not long before she'd met Kurt, who had lavished her with attention and compliments and praise, much like her beloved dad had done. And then there was the fact that her mother had taken a dislike to Kurt at first sight, making Dani all the more determined to date him, to her chagrin now.

She'd gone into her relationship with Kurt a spoiled, pampered, overly dependent and somewhat insecure girl. She had emerged wary, disillusioned and deeply discontented with who she had become. Only now was she building a life that she could truly take pride in, becoming more like the strong, independent, self-confident woman she wanted to be. Was it any wonder this thing with Teague scared her half-witless?

All in all, it was a good thing he wasn't looking for anything permanent. She should probably start being a little more careful, keeping a bit more distance between them, so she wouldn't be hurt too badly when it ended. As it would end.

It would be a lot easier to achieve that distance once school started again, she decided. Once her lessons were back in full swing. She was usually quite busy with her own pursuits and was quite capable of entertaining herself when she wasn't busy, she assured herself, reaching for a book she'd been meaning to read for months.

She was only a few pages into the novel when that all-too-familiar rap sounded on her door. She had jumped to her feet before she'd realized it, the book tossed carelessly aside. Exasperated with herself for reacting like one of Pavlov's dogs to the sound of Teague's knock, she took her time getting to the door, waiting until he'd knocked a second time to open it.

"Oh," she said, as if she hadn't been completely aware of who'd summoned her. "Hi, Teague. What's up?"

His hair damp and his cheeks reddened from the cold, light mist that was falling outside, he shrugged inside his leather jacket, shifting the scarf she wasn't sure he'd taken off since she'd given it to him. "Just got home from work. Listen, Dani, I'm sure it's too late to ask you this, but do you already have plans for tomorrow night?"

New Year's Eve. She had been invited to a couple of parties, and had politely declined both invitations because neither had appealed to her. She'd decided she would rather stay home and watch old movies than go out with men she didn't really want to see the new year in with.

"Um, no. I was planning to just stay home this year. Why?"

"There's this party," he said with a grimace. "I didn't think I was going to be available to attend, but it looks like I'll be free after all. I hate going to those things alone, but I thought if by some chance you could go with me… Not as a date, really," he added hastily. "Just a companion. But if you prefer not to go out, I'd understand."

She remembered her resolution to put more distance between them. Her vow that his puppy-dog eyes would never get to her again. And yet, here he stood, all tough and unshaven and leather clad and puppy-dog-eyed, and darned if she didn't hear herself blurting, "Okay. I guess I'll go, if you want someone to keep you company. Not a date."

His face lightened. "That's great. It's not a formal thing. Just party clothes. And we don't have to stay long if we aren't having a good time. I just need to make an appearance to keep my friends placated."

"Are you sure you wouldn't rather go on your own?" she couldn't help asking. "I mean, there could be some interesting singles there."

He shook his head firmly. "I'm not looking for a New Year's Eve fling this year. I've been working my tail off lately, and I just want to be sociable for a couple hours and then come home and crash, you know? That's why I figured I'd ask you. You'd understand."

In other words she wouldn't make too many demands on him, since they were only friends. Because that was exactly the way she wanted him to think of them, she couldn't imagine why his words left her feeling a little deflated. "What time?"

"I'll pick you up at eight," he said, motioning wryly toward his door across the hall. "Now I've got some calls to make, so I'll let you get back to what you were doing. See you tomorrow, okay?"

She closed her door and then sagged against it. Okay, she thought, trying to mentally regroup. So she was going to a New Year's Eve party with Teague. That didn't change any of the things she had thought earlier, or the vows she had made to herself. It just meant she had to decide what she was going to wear, she thought, moving toward her bedroom.

She was ready ten minutes early the next evening, and even that was a sign she'd changed in the past year or so, Dani decided, studying her reflection in satisfaction. There had been a time when she was always late, primping and obsessing about her appearance until everyone else had almost despaired of her showing up at all.

Even having streamlined her preparations, she thought she looked good tonight. She'd left her hair down, brushing it to a shiny, wavy curtain to her shoulders. Her makeup was a bit more dramatic than usual, a little extra glitter on the eyes and cheeks and lips in honor of the holiday.

There had been a time when she would have felt the need to rush out and buy something new for a party, but she'd refused to do so this time, choosing instead an outfit she had worn several times before, though not for this crowd. The black-and-silver halter top fit as though it had been specially tailored for her, and loose-legged black evening pants made her legs look even longer than usual, especially combined with heeled black and silver sandals. Fastening a pair of cascading silver earrings to her lobes, she resisted an impulse to fuss a little more with her hair, and turned firmly away from the mirror.

She carried a sparkling silver tote with her into the living room, along with a soft black wrap to keep her bare shoulders and back warm on the way to the party. It occurred to her only then that she didn't even know where they were going or who was hosting the event. Teague had asked, and she'd accepted without any questions. As simple as that.

Despite the plans she had made to spend New Year's Eve alone, and despite her reservations about getting too involved with Teague, she still found herself looking forward to the evening. She had always loved parties, and especially New Year's Eve parties. Loud music and cheery conversation, party favors and munchies, the traditional countdown to midnight—and the traditional kiss that followed, she added with a swallow. She hadn't wanted to kiss in the new year with either of the other men who'd asked her this year, but she wouldn't mind so much sharing a midnight embrace with Teague. It didn't have to mean anything serious, but it would certainly be something to look forward to.

Eight o'clock came and passed. Surprised that he was late, since it seemed out of character for him, she paced a little, hoping nothing was wrong. He knocked at a quarter after eight, and she made herself walk slowly to the door, not wanting him to think she'd been too anxious.

She knew something was wrong at the first sight of him. He wore jeans and his FBI jacket over a gray pullover. Something about the way the jacket draped made her think he was armed beneath it. The grim look on his face told her what he was going to say.

"You have to cancel," she said before he had the chance.

He nodded regretfully. "Something's going down on the job and I've been called in. I've got to run."

"Then go," she said, motioning toward the stairs. "And be careful, okay?"

"I'm sorry, Dani. Damn, you look good. I'll make this up to you, I promise."

She shook her head. "I was doing *you* the favor by going with you, remember? I'll be fine. Now, go. Don't let me keep you."

"Yeah, I've got to hurry. See you later."

"Bye, Teague."

He started to move away, then suddenly turned and reached out for her, snagging a hand at the back of her neck. His mouth was on hers, hard, before she had a chance to prepare herself.

The kiss didn't last much longer than a heartbeat, but she was still shaken by the intensity of it.

"Happy New Year," Teague murmured when he released her. And then he turned and hurried away without looking back at her. Which was just as well, she thought, afraid he would have seen just how strongly affected she had been by that brief, powerful kiss.

"Happy New Year," Rachel said when Dani answered the phone the next afternoon.

"Thank you. You, too. And tell Mark I said the same to him. I've already talked to Mother and Grandma."

"So, did you celebrate last night? Go to any great parties?"

Dani hesitated a moment before answering candidly, "Actually, I got all dressed up to go to a party and got stood up at the last moment. It wasn't his fault…he was called to work, but it was sort of a let-down."

"Teague?"

"Yes. We'd decided, sort of at the last minute, to go to a party—you know, just as friends—but after he had to bail, I just spent the evening watching old movies and pigging out on ice cream and the last of Mom's Christmas cookies. It wasn't too bad, actually."

"I guess you were really mad at Teague," Rachel said carefully.

"I told you, he couldn't help it. He had to work."

"Wow. That's interesting."

Dani lifted her eyebrows. "What's interesting?"

"Oh, you know. That you're so calm about the whole thing. I know how you hate having your plans changed at the last minute."

"How I *used* to hate things like that," Dani corrected impatiently. "I keep telling you I've grown up, but you still try to see me as the spoiled cheerleader from high school."

"No, I don't," Rachel argued firmly. "I know you've grown up a lot. We both have, I guess, since Dad died. I'm very proud of all you've accomplished this past year."

"Thanks, Ray-Ray," Dani said, oddly touched by the compliment. "I'm proud of you, too, you know."

She had always looked up to her older sister. It was only recently that she'd realized exactly how much Rachel had done to hold the family together during that dark period after their father had died.

"Here's to a successful new year for both of us," Rachel said softly.

"I'll drink to that," Dani said, lifting her canned diet soda with a smile, even though her sister couldn't see her.

Teague was on his way out on a Saturday afternoon in late January when he saw Mrs. Parsons step off the elevator with two rather large bags of groceries. He hurried to help her, taking the bags so she could unlock her door.

"Thank you, dear," she said, smiling sweetly up at him. "Why don't you come in and have a slice of pie, if you have time. It's cherry. I made it yesterday."

He hesitated only a moment. "Well, I've got a meeting later this afternoon, but I guess I've got time for a slice of pie," he said, giving in to temptation.

Obviously pleased, she led him to the kitchen. She put away the groceries while he ate his pie and drank a glass of iced tea from the pitcher she always kept filled in her refrigerator. He didn't have to worry about trying to talk with his mouth full; she chattered away the entire time, telling him all about her visit with her son. Though he'd already heard some of her stories, he listened attentively, knowing how much she enjoyed company.

"I haven't seen much of Dani since I got back," she complained. "She's been so busy. Have you seen her?"

"Only in passing a couple of times. She's swamped with classes and lessons right now, I guess." He had actually wondered if Dani was avoiding him for some reason. She hadn't seemed at all annoyed that he'd had to stand her up for the New Year's Eve party, but she certainly had been scarce around here since.

He could still remember so clearly how she had looked standing in her doorway in her sparkly party clothes, her eyes alight with anticipation of the evening out. It had taken all the willpower he had to walk away from her, allowing himself only one kiss.

The image of her standing there had haunted his dreams— waking and sleeping—ever since.

"I understand you and Dani spent quite a bit of time together while I was away," Mrs. Parsons said, giving him an impish look. "You went home for Thanksgiving with her, didn't you?"

"I did," he agreed, "but there was a reason for that."

"Yes, Hannah told me. I have to admit I'm glad I wasn't

here." She put a hand over her heart. "Just the thought of seeing you bloody and beaten makes me ill. I'm so glad you've recovered well. I hope you're being more careful now."

"Trying to be."

"Good. So, about you and Dani—"

"We're still just friends, Mrs. Parsons," he said gently. "After what we just talked about, you should understand why I'd have reservations about getting into a relationship with anyone, considering the demands of my job."

"You're telling me there aren't any married FBI agents?" she demanded, placing her gnarled hands on her hips.

"Well, yeah, there are a few," he admitted. "It's tough on them, though."

"Well, of course it is. Who ever said marriage was easy— for anyone? My late husband was an accountant. I didn't see him from January 1 until April 16. Let me tell you, I got tired of spending our March thirtieth wedding anniversaries watching him run figures after dinner. Caused us some problems through the years, but we learned to work around his schedule."

Teague shook his head and handed her his empty dessert plate. "Why are we discussing marriage, anyway? I'm certainly in no hurry to get married. And if you're thinking about Dani, I don't think she is, either. She considers herself a very independent and self-sufficient woman who doesn't want to tie herself down to anyone while she's getting her career established."

"Of course she does. I was an independent and self-sufficient woman, myself. I had a career, you know. I retired as a branch manager of a local bank. I had a lot of responsibility and worked some fairly long hours, but that didn't stop me from keeping my family together."

"I never knew you were in banking," he said.

She nodded vigorously. "There weren't a lot of women managers when I was promoted, but I never let that hold me back. Once I set my mind to something I wanted, I usually got it."

He couldn't imagine why that statement made him a little bit nervous.

Maybe it was the lack of sunshine, the lousy, cold, wet weather, the knowledge that spring was still so far away. Or maybe it was her own inner conflicts, but Dani grew increasingly tense as January slipped away and February began. It seemed that romance was everywhere she looked, in decorations and ads, TV programs and movies. And every time she saw a string of red hearts or heard a sappy love song, she found herself thinking of Teague. And that just annoyed her.

She was avoiding him, no question. She figured he knew it, since he looked at her so quizzically when their paths did cross. But this was the only way she knew to handle her tangled feelings for him. All she needed was a little distance, she assured herself. Just to get past all these sappy holidays and back to her comfortable routines.

Still, though she deliberately stayed too busy to spend much time with him, she discreetly kept tabs on him. She knew when he worked extralong hours, when his schedule was lighter, when he was gone on what she assumed— hoped?—were overnight assignments. He left town only once during those weeks, for a couple of days, and he let her know in passing beforehand that he would be gone. Just so she wouldn't worry, he had added, watching her closely as if to see if there was a chance that she would worry about him.

So when he suddenly disappeared during the first week of February, she did worry. She had seen him leave that afternoon, and he'd stopped to chat with her for a few minutes. He hadn't said a word about going out of town. He hadn't been carrying a bag, and he hadn't indicated that he was involved in a particularly time-consuming case.

By the third day she was practically stalking his apartment, waiting for some sign of him. She couldn't help remembering how he had looked when he'd collapsed into her arms that week of Thanksgiving, so badly injured and so determined to keep going. What if he was hurt again? What if he'd been injured—or worse—in the course of a case?

What if he was lying in a hospital room somewhere? No one would think to notify his neighbors, most likely. Why would they? It wasn't as if he had her listed as someone to call in case of an emergency. He could actually be dead, and she wouldn't know it unless she heard it on the news or found out by accident when someone came to clean out his apartment, she realized sickly.

Mrs. Parsons kept telling her that Teague was probably fine, that they surely would have heard if anything was wrong, but Dani could tell that the older woman was worried about him, too. She heard Mrs. Parsons's door open regularly, as if she were checking for signs of Teague almost as often as Dani was.

By the fourth day, Dani was ready to start making calls. She had to know something, she thought desperately. She wasn't going to sleep soundly until she was sure he was all right.

The problem was, she didn't know who to call. He had never told her his stepmother's name, or where in Florida she lived. She didn't know any of his friends or co-workers, having missed the party. So, should she just look up FBI in the phone book? Ask whoever answered if an agent named Teague McCauley happened to be lying in a hospital somewhere?

She was pacing her living room when she heard someone

out in the hallway. Somehow recognizing Teague's steps, she threw open the door. "Where the *hell* have you been?"

Teague was tired. All-the-way-to-the-bone tired. So exhausted that he couldn't even make himself stand up straight when Dani stormed out of her apartment like a madwoman.

"I've been working," he said, hearing his words slur a little as they emerged. "Got caught up in a case that took me out of the state for a few days."

He needed a shower, a shave, a hot meal and a good night's sleep. Not necessarily in that order. And, as lovely as she always was, Dani was standing squarely between him and his door, behind which he could find all of those things.

Her hands were planted—fisted, really—on her hips as she glared at him. Her eyes were narrowed, darkened almost to navy, her mouth turned downward in displeasure. He'd still like to kiss that fabulous mouth, frown or no, but first he had to get some rest. It would be incredibly embarrassing to fall asleep right in the middle of a kiss.

Realizing she was speaking again in a low, tight voice, he tried to pay attention. "In all of that time, you couldn't find two minutes to call me and tell me you were all right?" she asked.

"No, I really couldn't," he replied with a faint shrug. "I figured you would know I was working."

"How was I to know that? For all I knew, you were off on a pleasure trip. Or lying in a hospital bed somewhere. Or…or something else."

"As you can see, I'm fine. Thanks for your concern, but now I…"

"Thanks for my concern?" she repeated in disbelief. "That's it?"

The strain of the past few days was fast catching up with

him. He really wasn't in any shape to be having this conversation. "Look, Dani, what do you want? I said I'm sorry you were worried. But for all I knew, you never even noticed I was gone."

"Wouldn't you have noticed if I had just disappeared for days at a time?"

"I'd notice," he snapped back. "I would just figure it was none of my business where you were."

He realized that hadn't come out quite right when she gasped and stiffened. "You're right," she said flatly. "It is absolutely none of my business where you go or why."

Gripping the back of his neck with one hand, he grimaced. "That's not what I meant. You're the one who's made it clear you want to keep everything all casual and undefined between us. I never know from one day to the next whether you'll even deign to talk to me again, much less…well, anything else. Either we're a couple or we're not, but I'll be damned if I'll be one of your pathetically eager puppies, hanging around hoping for a crumb of attention from you."

Okay, that hadn't been his smoothest speech, either. And judging from her expression, it had not been at all well received.

"Fine," she said. "You want a tidy, one-word definition? Try this one. *Over.*"

"Dani—"

She was already storming back through her open door. She slammed it closed before he could say anything else.

"Damn it," he growled, only then noticing that Mrs. Parsons's door was also ajar.

The older woman gave him a look of sympathy. "Get some rest, dear," she advised quietly. "You both need to cool down before you talk again."

"Something tells me Dani won't be cooling off that much for the next decade or so," he muttered, his shoulders sagging.

"You heard her. Whatever we had, it's over. And maybe that's for the best."

"Get some rest," his neighbor said again. "I'm sure everything will look different tomorrow."

But Teague didn't think so. It seemed to him that Dani had been looking for a reason to end it between them from the beginning, even before anything had really gotten started. She'd tried to control him, and when that hadn't worked out, she'd dumped him. Well, fine, he thought, stripping off his clothes and stumbling into the shower. If it was over, it was over. He'd been expecting this all along, anyway.

He just hadn't expected it to hurt quite this much, he thought, letting his head droop beneath the steady stream of hot water.

Chapter Thirteen

Dani was thinking about moving. Her lease was coming up at the end of March and it seemed like a good time for a change of scenery. She wasn't running away from Teague, she assured herself. She'd hardly caught a glimpse of him since their quarrel a week earlier, anyway, though she knew he'd been home most every day since.

He was very good at avoiding her.

It would be nice to find an apartment with a somewhat larger kitchen. Now that she'd started cooking, she was rather enjoying it, and her current kitchen was really too small to store some of the appliances she'd like to buy eventually. And it would be nice to have an apartment with an outside entrance, maybe a nice little courtyard. She had never intended to stay here permanently.

It wasn't about Teague, she assured herself again. Not entirely, anyway.

Sure, she'd had a good cry the night they'd…well, *broken up* didn't seem like the right term, since they'd never really been together. The night they'd ended their "friendship with benefits." She'd been hurt and insulted by some of the things he had said, and it was only natural that there'd been a few tears. And that she'd almost cried once or twice since, just remembering how cutting their quarrel had been, even after they'd spent so many pleasant hours together.

Hadn't she known all along that the ending wouldn't be easy between them?

She would get over this, she vowed. She'd never expected anything to come of it, anyway. Hadn't even wanted anything to, really. Falling in love, getting serious, making a commitment just wasn't on her life schedule right now. So if she burst into tears at hearing James Blunt wail, "Goodbye, My Lover," it had to be due to hormones, not a broken heart. She turned off the radio just as he sang, "Goodbye, my friend." Wiping her eyes, she got out her music history books, determined to lose herself in her studies.

She was locked into her apartment on February 13th—not hiding, just studying, she assured herself—wrapped in an afghan to protect her from the chill that seeped through the old windows of the building. It was bitterly cold out, and a nasty winter storm was predicted for the next day. She didn't know if Teague was working tonight in this terrible weather, but she reminded herself that she didn't really care. As he had coolly pointed out, it was really none of her business.

A knock on her door brought her quickly to her feet. Even as she moved to answer it, she realized that it wasn't Teague's knock. Sure enough, Mrs. Parsons stood on the other side of the door. Dani tried to convince herself that she was relieved.

"I was in the mood to make brownies today, so I brought

you some," Mrs. Parsons said, holding out a covered plate. "I know you have a weakness for chocolate."

"Yes, I do. Which makes it very naughty of you to bring it to me," Dani teased, accepting the plate anyway.

"Wouldn't hurt you to gain a few pounds," the older woman said with a bluntness that was certainly familiar to Dani, considering the way her mother and grandmother always spoke their minds.

"Considering that I'll probably lick this plate clean, you might just see that happen. Would you like to come in? Can I get you anything to drink?"

"Nothing to drink, but I wouldn't mind coming in for a minute."

Setting the brownies on a table, Dani waited until her visitor was seated before settling on the sofa herself. "Have you decided yet about whether you're going to accept your son's invitation to move into his guest house?"

Mrs. Parsons nodded. "I believe I will," she said. "It's been a hard decision, but I finally made up my mind today. I called him just before dinner. He sounded pleased."

"I'm sure he is. He must look forward to having you closer to him where he can see you every day."

Mrs. Parsons laughed wryly. "We'll see if he still feels that way after I've been there awhile."

"I have no doubt that he will. I'll miss you, though."

"I'll miss you, too, dear. I think very highly of you, you know. Like a favorite niece."

Dani blinked, wondering why tears seemed to hover so close these days. Maybe she needed to start taking some vitamins or something. "That's very sweet."

"Now, tell me about you and Teague. When are the two of you going to make up and be friends again?"

This, too, sounded like something her older relatives would ask. She decided to handle the personal question from Mrs. Parsons just as she would from one of her own family. Candidly, but making it clear that she wasn't really looking for advice. "Teague and I both have very busy lives, Mrs. Parsons. It's better if we just go our separate ways for now."

Clucking her tongue in disapproval, the older woman shook her head. "You're both so stubborn. It's obvious that you're both unhappy with the way things stand between you, but neither one of you will do a thing about it."

"I know you heard the things he and I said to each other that night last week. We were both pretty mad when we parted."

"One quarrel and you're ready to give up?" Mrs. Parsons shook her head again. "If you'd heard the spats my husband and I got into during all our years together, and knew how happy we were together despite those arguments, you'd know how foolish that sounds."

"Yes, well, this is different. Teague and I aren't— We don't— We didn't have that sort of relationship."

"Hmm. Maybe you could have, if you'd just worked at it a little. But that's none of my affair, of course," she said quickly, before Dani could point out that obvious fact. "I just hate to see you both unhappy, when I've grown so fond of you both."

"I'm not unhappy, Mrs. Parsons," Dani lied without blinking.

She might as well have tried to fool one of her too-percep- tive relatives. Mrs. Parsons gave her a look that said a great deal, and then rose from her chair. "I'd better get back home. It's getting close to time for my favorite television program."

Dani walked her to the door. "Thanks again for the brownies."

"You're welcome. Good night, dear."

Closing the door, Dani stood where she was for several long minutes, wondering if Mrs. Parsons was right. Was

Teague really unhappy with the way things had ended between them? She doubted that he was hurting quite as badly as she was, but maybe he regretted some of the things they had said to each other. It just seemed too late to even try to go back to the way things had been between them before those words had been spoken, she thought with a long, deep sigh.

The storm hit as predicted the next evening. By 10:00 p.m., everything outside was covered in a half inch of ice. Dani was watching the weather reports on her TV when the electricity in the building suddenly went out. She figured a few tree limbs somewhere had collapsed beneath the pressure of the ice and fallen over some lines. According to the reports she'd heard before she'd lost power, it was happening all around the area.

She groped for the flashlight she'd kept handy, just in case. It wouldn't be long before she'd feel the cold, since the building was heated by electricity. She wrapped her afghan around the shoulders of the warm turtleneck sweater she wore with her jeans, and was glad she'd kept her boots on over her thick socks.

Some Valentine's Day this was turning out to be, she thought glumly. It felt almost as if the weather was responding to the stormy mood she had been in for the past week. Something told her she was never going to enjoy this holiday again, as it would always remind her of Teague, and how much it hurt to be this bitterly estranged from him.

Trying to distract herself again from that painful subject, she thought suddenly of Mrs. Parsons, sitting alone next door in the dark and the cold. Wearing the afghan like a shawl, she made her way toward her door by the beam of her flashlight, feeling the need to make sure the older woman was all right.

The hallway was deserted on their wing, though she could hear voices coming from the apartments on the other side of the elevator. She didn't think Hannah was home. Probably staying with one of her study friends. She didn't know whether Teague was in or not, but his door opened just as she reached Mrs. Parsons's apartment.

"Are you okay?" he asked, recognizing her in the dim glow of her flashlight.

"Yes," she answered briefly. "Are you?"

"Yeah. Have you checked with Mrs. Parsons yet?"

"No. I was trying to decide whether to knock. If she's already asleep, I wouldn't want to wake her. I'm afraid she would fall over something in the darkness."

He stepped out of his apartment into the hallway, little more than a deeper shadow in the darkness that was barely affected by Dani's little flashlight. "Good point. The power could be out for a while, though, since the crews have all they can handle tonight with the power out all over town. We need to make sure Mrs. P. is going to stay warm enough for the night."

"Maybe we should call her. I know she keeps a telephone by her bed."

"Good idea."

But before either of them could make a move, Mrs. Parsons's door opened. "Oh, thank goodness," she said, her voice quavering. "I thought I heard you two out here."

Mrs. Parsons, too, held a flashlight, and Dani noted immediately that it wasn't quite steady. "Are you okay?" she asked again.

"I'm just so glad to see you both. Well, I can't really see you, but I'm glad to know you're here."

Dani heard Teague take a quick step forward, responding to the uncharacteristic anxiety in the older woman's voice. "What's wrong? Are you hurt?"

"No." Mrs. Parsons gave a sheepish laugh. "Just a bit

anxious. I don't like the dark. I usually keep a night-light burning. But it's so black in here now, without even a glow from the security lights outside."

Dani spoke sympathetically, her tone reassuring. "It's okay, Mrs. Parsons. I'll stay with you until the lights come back on, if you like."

"Could you both come in? Just for a little while?" The tiniest quaver shook her voice as she asked. "I'd just feel better having us all together for a bit."

Dani looked uncertainly at Teague, whose expression was hidden in shadows. But she saw him nod. "Let me grab a few things and I'll be right there," he said.

"Oh, thank you, dear." Mrs. Parsons reached out to clutch Dani's arm, as if to make sure she didn't slip away in the meantime. "We'll wait for you inside."

As they entered the apartment, Dani ran the beam of her flashlight around the living room, satisfying herself that everything was in place. She was glad that Mrs. Parsons had kept a flashlight nearby so she hadn't tripped over anything in the darkness. Turning her beam in the vicinity of her neighbor while trying not to blind her with the light, she realized that the older woman wore a thick, long robe, probably over a warm nightgown. "Had you already gone to bed?"

"I had just climbed into bed. I was tired, but I wanted to check the weather one last time before I turned in. I'm usually fast asleep by now."

"Maybe you should try going back to bed. If you pile on the covers, you should stay warm enough until morning."

"Yeah, go on to bed, Mrs. P. Dani and I will hang out in here for a while, until we're sure everything's okay." Teague entered the open door as he spoke, visible only as a dark shape behind his flashlight.

"I am very tired." Again, Mrs. Parsons's voice was a bit unsteady. "I usually turn in an hour earlier than this."

"Let me help you get back into bed," Dani volunteered, moving toward her. "Where do you keep your extra blankets?"

"In the bedroom closet." Mrs. Parsons clutched Dani's arm as they made their way carefully to the other room. She seemed to Dani to be smaller than usual, a little more fragile. "I really appreciate this. I'm sorry to be so much trouble."

"You're no trouble at all," Dani assured her. "I'd just be sitting in the dark in my apartment rather than yours."

"You and Teague certainly don't have to sit up with me all night. But if you could stay for just a while, until I'm asleep...maybe an hour or so?"

"I'll certainly stay. My flashlight is bright enough to let me read by it, so I can entertain myself. Teague will be right across the hall, if we need him. There's no reason for him to sit with me." She intended to send him home as soon as she got Mrs. Parsons settled, and she doubted that he would argue with her. She was sure he was no more inclined to spend an hour in the darkness with her than she was with him after their last encounter. She couldn't imagine a more awkward situation.

"I'm being silly, I know," Mrs. Parsons said. "It just feels better knowing there are other people in the house during times like this."

Dani had never seen her independent and seemingly self-sufficient neighbor this anxious. She supposed it was a good thing, after all, that Mrs. Parsons would be moving closer to her son soon. Perhaps age was finally starting to take its toll on the sweet lady.

Leaving Mrs. Parsons snuggled under a pile of warm blankets, Dani carefully moved back into the living room, bumping her shin only once during the path. Mrs. Parsons certainly did like large, heavy furniture, she thought ruefully, limping the rest of the way.

"You okay?" Teague stood next to a living room table, where he had just lit an emergency candle in a heavy jar. A second candle was already burning on the coffee table, casting enough light in the room that Dani could make her way to the couch without the use of her flashlight.

"Yeah. I just hit my leg on a chest in the hallway. I have a feeling there will be a bruise, but no lasting damage."

He was pulling something out of a canvas bag as she spoke. "You want a cup of coffee? It's decaf, so it won't keep you awake all night, but it'll help keep you warm."

"You brought coffee?"

He shrugged. "I'd just made a pot when the power went out. I poured it into a thermos, so it's still hot. I grabbed a couple of mugs out of Mrs. P.'s kitchen. I didn't think she'd mind."

"I'm sure she wouldn't." Dani accepted a steaming mug from him and took a sip. The warm beverage tasted good and felt even better as it seeped into her. He hadn't had to ask if she took it black. He knew she did, just as she knew he took his the same way.

Her chest tightening with the memories of the cozy cups of coffee they had enjoyed together, she lowered the mug and spoke a bit gruffly. "There's no need for you to sit here with me, you know. I'm just going to stay until I'm sure she's sleeping comfortably, and then I'll go back to my own place."

But Teague had already settled into a chair, a mug cradled between his hands. "I'll stay until I finish my coffee. Hate to leave you in the dark by yourself with nothing to do."

"Thanks to your candles, I'm not completely in the dark," she reminded him. "And if I get too bored, I have my MP3 player in my sweater pocket."

"I know my company can't compete with your obsession with the Foo Fighters, but I'll stay for a few minutes anyway."

Another subtle reminder that he had gotten to know her quite well during the past few months. How had that happened, anyway? She'd tried so hard to keep it all light and casual, and yet somehow he had crept into her life, her thoughts. Her heart, she reluctantly added with a ripple of fear.

After a few moments of silence, Teague spoke again. "Look, Dani, about what I said last week—"

"Forget it," she said quickly, dreading a postmortem of that quarrel. "I was out of line asking where you'd been. Let's just drop it, okay?"

"You weren't out of line. Just sending mixed signals. Either we have the sort of relationship where we check in with each other or we don't. You can't have it both ways, expecting me to report in to you while I'm not allowed to even express my concerns for your safety when you come in alone late at night."

She winced, because what he'd described was so painfully accurate. That was exactly the way she had treated him. "I'm sorry. I had no right to jump you like that when you came home. I was worried when you disappeared for so long, and I overreacted."

"And I was dead tired and grouchy, and I snarled at you. I should have thanked you, instead, for being concerned. And apologized for alarming you. Had I known you'd be that worried, I would have found a way to get a message to you somehow."

"How on earth could you not have known I'd be worried?" she asked incredulously. "Teague, you just disappeared for days with no warning. And so soon after you'd been beaten up so badly you could hardly stand. I was sure you were dead in some alley somewhere or lying in some ICU unit with a gunshot wound or something terrible like that. I could hardly sleep the whole time because of the horrible scenarios I kept coming up with."

He took a moment to digest that, and she worried that she had revealed too much with her frazzled ramblings. "You see," he said finally, "I have quite a few friends. A bunch of them were at the party we were supposed to attend on New Year's Eve. I didn't call them that night to tell them I had to work. I figured they'd know. I didn't call any of them this time, either. I can't take the time whenever I get called away on a big case to call all my friends and let them know I may be gone for a few days. It happens fairly often, which is why I keep a packed bag in my car at all times."

She was glad then for the shadows that she hoped hid her reddened cheeks from him. He was making her feel very foolish about her outburst that night he'd returned home—as if she hadn't already regretted that scene a hundred times or more.

"Now, it would be different," he continued, "if I had someone special in my life. Someone who was more than just one of my many friends and acquaintances. Someone who had every right to worry about me and to be reassured, when possible, that everything was okay."

Her fingers tightened around the mug. Was he speaking metaphorically or…? "Well, sure, I guess, um…"

Her incoherent stammering barely seemed to register with him as he spoke on. "The thing is, it's hard being involved with someone in my job, Dani. We've discussed it before. I've explained that I've generally avoided serious relationships because I wasn't sure I would ever find anyone who could deal with what I do. It would take someone pretty damned special. Someone with a satisfying life and strong interests of her own. Someone who wouldn't expect me to give up the job I love, but would be there to welcome me when I get home.

Someone I would want to support just as enthusiastically. Say, by attending her concerts and recitals whenever I'm available to do so."

Okay, now that was making it personal. She gulped. "What are you saying, Teague?" she asked bluntly.

"I guess what I'm saying is that I've been miserable this past week. I miss you, Dani. This wasn't what I planned. I tried to fight it, tried to convince myself I could be with you without falling for you—but it didn't work. I'm hooked. You can reel me in or let me go, but I just needed you to know I'm tugging on the line."

The whole fishing analogy threw her for a minute, but she quickly reminded herself that Teague wasn't the type to make flowery declarations. What he was saying was clear enough. "Friends with benefits" wasn't what he wanted from her anymore.

There, in the candlelit dimness of her neighbor's fussy living room, she sat with her hands clenched around the warm mug, stunned by Teague's unexpected words, trying to decide how to respond. He gave her plenty of time, making no further sound and moving only to lift his own mug to his lips, as if his speech had left his mouth dry.

"Oh, for pity's sake, Dani, tell him how you feel," Mrs. Parsons called out impatiently from the other room. "Don't just leave him sitting there in suspense."

Dani was startled into a gasp, having forgotten all about the older woman, and totally unaware that their conversation had been audible to her. Mrs. Parsons must have been shamelessly eavesdropping the whole time. Teague looked just as chagrined. Even in the flickering glow of the candles, Dani could tell that his cheeks had darkened a little in response to the knowledge that his awkward declaration had been overheard.

Because the thought of tough, self-assured Agent Sexy blushing made her melt a little inside, she found the courage to say quietly, "I'm reeling."

The word had several meanings, all of which applied at that moment. But Teague seemed to understand immediately what she was telling him. He set his mug on the nearest table and rose to his feet. And though her heart was beating so hard she could hardly breathe, Dani did the same.

She wasn't sure which one of them moved first, but suddenly they were locked together, Teague's mouth hard on hers. It felt as if months had passed since he had last kissed her, and she kissed him back as if she'd been starving for his touch. Which, of course, she had been, as much as she had tried to deny it even to herself.

After giving them a few moments of privacy, Mrs. Parsons called out again. "You two can go now. I'd like to get some sleep. Be sure to lock the door when you leave."

The smug satisfaction in her voice made both Dani and Teague frown.

"You little conniver," Teague said, looking toward that darkened bedroom. "You weren't afraid at all, were you?"

"Good night, dear. Don't forget to blow out those candles when you leave. Fire hazard, you know."

Muttering beneath his breath in a mixture of amusement and dismay, Teague blew out the candles, plunging the room into darkness. Gripping Dani's arm, he led her to the door by the beam of his flashlight, leaving the coffee and mugs behind. She gave a fleeting thought to them, but figured she would collect them tomorrow. They had more important things to concentrate on for now, she thought with a nervous swallow.

Teague took her to her apartment. She'd left the door ajar in her haste to check on her neighbor, but he didn't even bother to fuss at her for her lax security this time. He merely escorted her inside and booted the door closed behind them.

There weren't any candles burning now, and his flashlight was only in the way. She had left hers at Mrs. Parsons's, she remembered belatedly, but even that didn't seem important now. Teague set the flashlight on a table, barely illuminating their faces when he gripped her forearms and gazed down at her in the shadows.

"You're willing to give this a real try?" he asked, as if to make sure he had understood her correctly. "No pulling back this time?"

"I'm still nervous about it," she admitted. "I mean, my last relationship was such a monumental disaster…."

"I keep telling you, Dani, I'm nothing like that guy Kurt. But that's not what you're really worried about, is it?" he asked suddenly, as though the realization had just hit him. "You're more worried that *you're* the same person you were with him."

She nodded numbly.

"That," he told her, tugging her into his arms, "is just crazy. I don't know exactly what went on between the two of you back then, but the Dani Madison I know would never let any man put her down or control her. And if any guy ever raised a hand to her now, she'd leave him bleeding on the floor."

"I want to believe that's true," she murmured, "but I can't deny that I've become pretty well obsessed with you. I think about you all the time, Teague. I swore I'd never be that way again with another man. Maybe I haven't changed as much as I want to believe."

Her candor seemed to disarm him for a moment, leaving him speechless and her feeling extremely vulnerable about whatever he might say next. When he spoke, his voice wasn't entirely steady, which made her heart clench. "Don't you see,

Dani? I feel the same way about you. I haven't been able to stop thinking about you since the first time I saw you. Even when I'm concentrating completely on my job, you're always there, hovering at the back of my mind until I have a free minute to think about you again."

He cupped her face in his hand, his palm warm against her cold cheek. "It's not something I've had much experience with myself, but from what I've been told, a little obsession is all just a part of falling in love."

Her pulse rate jumped. "You—you're in love with me?"

"I'm pretty sure I am," he muttered. "Because I know I've never felt like this about anyone else before. Never thought it was worth taking this kind of risk with anyone else before."

"I've never felt like this before, either," she whispered. "What I felt for Kurt—that wasn't love. I never even knew him, really. This is so very different."

"You see?" he asked against her lips. "Everything's different now. You. Me. Us."

She wrapped her arms around his neck and pressed her mouth harder against his, demanding the kiss he'd been teasing her with. He willingly complied, kissing her until they were both trembling and panting, their bodies warm in the rapidly cooling apartment.

"It isn't going to be easy," he warned when he caught enough breath to speak.

"I don't need it to be easy," she replied unsteadily, pulling his head back down again. "I just need it to be honest. Real. Equal."

"All of that and more," he vowed, kissing her again.

Using his familiarity with her apartment layout, he began to nudge her toward her bedroom door. Her heart beat more quickly in anticipation of the pleasures to come. They had just stepped into the bedroom when the electricity came back on, flooding the room with sudden light.

Even as Dani blinked in disorientation, Teague shot out a hand to hit the light switch, making the room go dim again. "Let's just keep the rest of the world outside for a little while, shall we?" he asked, shutting the bedroom door.

She caught his hand and tugged him toward her. "I think it's going to be longer than a little while."

Laughing softly, he tumbled with her down onto the bed.

Epilogue

Nobody said relationships were supposed to be easy, Teague reminded himself as he walked into the kitchen of his house, still sweating from the heat of a blazing September day that had long since faded into an oppressively sultry night. He vaguely remembered being lectured by Mrs. Parsons, back when he'd been trying to analyze his feelings for Dani. His former neighbor had told him then that keeping a marriage together was hard, and that it required a lot of compromise and concessions.

Some of his friends and acquaintances had expressed concern that a union between a workaholic FBI agent and a one-time pampered princess would be extremely difficult, with her expecting more than he could give, and him forgetting to observe the little niceties that kept such a woman satisfied. Expect problems, he'd been told, sometimes subtly, sometimes quite bluntly. He should brace himself for the possibility of failure.

He had listened politely to all those warnings, he thought now, looking around the empty kitchen, but he hadn't let them dissuade him from marrying Dani after a whirlwind courtship. He'd been absolutely, rather naively, convinced that they could overcome whatever adversities life threw at them, that their love would be strong enough to weather the storms.

He had been uncharacteristically optimistic, blithely certain that he and Dani were meant to be together, firmly assured that they would find a way to hold their relationship together, even though so many others in his profession—in every profession, for that matter—fell apart beneath the strain of everyday aggravations.

Walking through the quiet hallways and up the empty stairs to the bedroom, he wondered now, as he sometimes did, what had made him so quick to believe that he and Dani would succeed where so many others had failed. It hadn't been at all like him to let his heart lead him when common sense tried to hold him back. It had been the only time in his adult life when he'd allowed himself to be a romantic fool, ignoring his deeply ingrained warnings of danger and rushing recklessly into unfamiliar terrain.

Shaking his head in bemusement at how foolishly love-struck he had been, he opened the bedroom door and stepped inside.

Dani sat in a little chair in front of the antique vanity she'd found at an estate sale, spreading a scented cream onto her arms, which were bared by the thin white summer nightgown that fell softly over her perfect curves. She jumped up with a gasp when he entered the room, and then rushed straight into his arms.

"I didn't even hear you come in," she scolded between eager kisses. "When did you get back?"

"Just now," he replied, pulling her more snugly against him, even though he was rumpled and sweaty and she was clean and rose scented. He figured they could take a shower together. Later. "I came straight up to find you."

"Aren't you hungry?" she asked, holding herself away from him for a moment.

"Starving," he assured her, and reached for the hem of her gown. It had been a long three days since he'd last seen her.

Laughing, she fell onto the bed with him. They had learned never to waste a moment of their time together. While they were perfectly capable of taking care of themselves when they were apart, it was times like these that recharged them, giving them strength and encouragement to face the demands of their very busy lives.

So maybe it wasn't always easy, Teague thought, losing himself in Dani's arms. Maybe it wasn't meant to be. But, despite anyone's reservations, including their own, he had been absolutely right: the love he and Dani had found together as friends and neighbors was well worth any effort it might take to keep it alive for a lifetime.

* * * * *

Love Inspired
HISTORICAL

*Powerful, engaging stories of romance, adventure and faith
set in the past—when life was simpler and faith played a
major role in everyday lives.*

*Turn the page for a sneak preview of
HIGH COUNTRY BRIDE
by Jillian Hart.*

*Love Inspired Historical—love and faith
throughout the ages*

Silence remained between them, and she felt the rake of his gaze, taking her in from the top of her wind-blown hair where escaped tendrils snapped in the wind to the toe of her scuffed, patched shoes. She watched him fist up his big, work-roughened hands and expected the worst.

"You never told me, Miz Nelson. Where are you going to go?" His tone was flat, his jaw tensed as if he were still fighting his temper. His blue gaze shot past her to watch the children going about their picking up.

"I don't know." Her throat went dry. Her tongue felt thick as she answered. "When I find employment, I could wire a payment to you. Rent. Y-you aren't think-ing of bringing the sher-rif in?"

"You think I want *payment?*" He boomed like winter thunder. *"You think I want rent money?"*

"Frankly, I don't know what you want."

"I'll tell you what I don't want. I don't want—" His words cannoned in the silence as he paused, and a passing pair of geese overhead honked in flat-noted tones. He grimaced, and it was impossible to know what he would say or do.

She trembled, not from fear of him, she truly didn't believe he would strike her, but from the unknown. Of being forced to take the frightening step off the only safe spot she'd known since she'd lost Pa's house.

When you were homeless, everything seemed so fragile, so easily off balance, for it was a big, unkind world for a woman alone with her children. She had no one to protect her. No one to care. The truth was, she'd never had those things in her husband. How could she expect them from any stranger? Especially this man she hardly knew, who was harsh and cold and hardhearted.

And, worse, what if he brought in the law?

"You can't keep living out of a wagon," he said, still angry, the cords still straining in his neck. "Animals have enough sense to keep their young cared for and safe."

Yes, it was as she'd thought. He intended to be as cruel about this as he could be. She spun on her heel, pulling up all her defenses, and was determined to let his upcoming hurtful words roll off her like rainwater on an oiled tarp. She grabbed the towel the children had neatly folded and tossed it into the laundry box in the back of the wagon.

"Miz Nelson. I'm talking to you."

"Yes, I know. If you expect me to stand there while you tongue lash me, you're mistaken. I have packing to get to." Her fingers were clumsy as she hefted the bucket of water she'd brought for washing—she wouldn't need that now—and heaved.

His hand clasped on the handle beside hers, and she could feel the life and power of him vibrate along the thin metal. "Give it to me."

Her fingers let go. She felt stunned as he walked away,

easily carrying the bucket that had been so heavy to her, and quietly, methodically, put out the small cooking fire. He did not seem as ominous or as intimidating—somehow—as he stood in the shadows, bent to his task, although she couldn't say why that was. Perhaps it was because he wasn't acting the way she was used to men acting. She was quite used to doing all the work.

Jamie scurried over, juggling his wooden horses, to watch. Daisy hung back, eyes wide and still, taking in the mysterious goings-on.

He is different when he's near to them, she realized. He didn't seem harsh, and there was no hint of anger—or, come to think of it, any other emotion—as he shook out the empty bucket, nodded once to the children and then retraced his path to her.

"Let me guess." He dropped the bucket onto the tailgate, and his anger appeared to be back. Cords strained in his neck and jaw as he growled at her. "If you leave here, you don't know where you're going and you have no money to get there with?"

She nodded. "Yes, sir."

"Then get you and your kids into the wagon. I'll hitch up your horses for you." His eyes were cold and yet they were not unfeeling as he fastened his gaze on hers. "I have an empty shanty out back of my house that no one's living in. You can stay there for the night."

"What?" She stumbled back, and the solid wood of the tailgate bit into the small of her back. "But—"

"There will be no argument," he bit out, interrupting her. "None at all. I buried a wife and son years ago, what was most precious to me, and to see you and them neglected like this—

with no one to care—" His jaw ground again and his eyes were no longer cold.

Joanna didn't think she'd ever seen anything sadder than Aiden McKaslin as the sun went down on him.

* * * * *

Don't miss this deeply moving story,
HIGH COUNTRY BRIDE,
available July 2008
from the new Love Inspired Historical line.

Also look for SEASIDE CINDERELLA
by Anna Schmidt,
where a poor servant girl and a wealthy merchant prince
might somehow make a life together.

REQUEST YOUR FREE BOOKS!
2 FREE NOVELS PLUS 2 FREE GIFTS!

SPECIAL EDITION®
Life, Love and Family!

YES! Please send me 2 FREE Silhouette Speäal Edition® novels and my 2 FREE gifts (gifts are worth about $10). After receiving them, if I don't wish to receive any more books, I can return the shipping statement marked "cancel." If I don't cancel, I will receive 6 brand-new novels every month and be billed just $4.24 per book in the U.S. or $4.99 per book in Canada, plus 25¢ shipping and handling per book and applicable taxes, if any*. That's a savings of at least 15% off the cover price! I understand that accepting the 2 free books and gifts places me under no obligation to buy anything. I can always return a shipment and cancel at any time. Even if I never buy another book from Silhouette, the two free books and gifts are mine to keep forever.

235 SDN EEYU 335 SDN EEY6

Name _____ (PLEASE PRINT) _____

Address _____ Apt. # _____

City _____ State/Prov. _____ Zip/Postal Code _____

Signature (if under 18, a parent or guardian must sign)

Mail to the Silhouette Reader Service:
IN U.S.A.: P.O. Box 1867, Buffalo, NY 14240-1867
IN CANADA: P.O. Box 609, Fort Erie, Ontario L2A 5X3

Not valid to current subscribers of Silhouette Speäal Edition books.

Want to try two free books from another line?
Call 1-800-873-8635 or visit www.morefreebooks.com.

* Terms and prices subject to change without notice. N.Y. residents add applicable sales tax. Canadian residents will be charged applicable provinäal taxes and GST. This offer is limited to one order per household. All orders subject to approval. Credit or debit balances in a customer's account(s) may be offset by any other outstanding balance owed by or to the customer. Please allow 4 to 6 weeks for delivery. Offer available while quantities last.

Your Privacy: Silhouette is committed to protecting your privacy. Our Privacy Policy is available online at www.eHarlequin.com or upon request from the Reader Service. From time to time we make our lists of customers available to reputable third parties who may have a product or service of interest to you. If you would prefer we not share your name and address, please check here. ☐

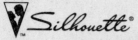

COMING NEXT MONTH

#1909 IN BED WITH THE BOSS—Christine Rimmer
Back in Business
Little did hotel-chain CFO Tom Holloway realize that his new
executive assistant spelled trouble. But even though single mom
Shelly Winston was planted by Holloway's worst enemy to take him
down, Shelly was no dupe—she had a mind of her own and an eye
for her handsome boss.

#1910 DIAMOND IN THE ROUGH—Marie Ferrarella
Kate's Boys
Sportswriter Mike Marlowe wasn't one to pull punches in his
newspaper column. So when his barbed commentary about a fallen
baseball idol caught the attention of the man's daughter, it meant
fireworks. Miranda Shaw would protect her father's name to the end—
but would she remember to protect her heart from the cagey scribe?

#1911 HER TEXAS LAWMAN—Stella Bagwell
Men of the West
When someone ran Lucita Sanchez off the highway, it was no accident,
but Chief Deputy Ripp McCleod was skeptical of the ranching
heiress's story. Soon two things became apparent—someone was
indeed stalking Lucita, and Ripp would do anything to protect her as
his interest in the case—and the woman—grew very personal....

#1912 THE BACHELOR'S STAND-IN WIFE—Susan Crosby
Wives for Hire
Stalwart bachelor David Falcon needed a woman to administer his
household—nothing more. His first mistake—if he wanted to stay
single!—was hiring down-on-her-luck Valerie Sinclair. Because in no
time flat, David was charmed by this woman and her eight-year-old
daughter. Now his bachelorhood teetered on the brink.

#1913 THE COWBOY'S LADY—Nicole Foster
The Brothers of Rancho Pintada
Bull rider Josh Garrett was reckless; shopkeeper Eliana Tamar was
responsible. But when fate threw these childhood friends back together,
it looked as if Eliana had what it took to tame the wild cowboy...until
Josh got a chance of a lifetime to win the title of his dreams. Could
Eliana compete with his first love—rodeo—after all?

#1914 THE LAST MAN SHE'D MARRY—Helen R. Myers
After being caught in the crossfire of a troubling case, Texas divorce
attorney Alyx Carmel went to regroup at her cousin's house in soothing
Sedona, Arizona. Where she ran smack-dab into sexy FBI agent
Jonas Hunter, a man she'd reluctantly turned her back on before.
But this time, he wasn't taking no for an answer....